SAECULUM

BOOK 1:

COLLAPSE

JOSHUA A. MORRIS, M.S.

Saeculum: Collapse is a work of fiction. Names, characters,
places, and incidents are either the product of the author's
imagination or are used fictitiously. Any resemblance to actual
persons, living or dead, events, or locations is entirely
coincidental.

To the Veterans of GWOT:

You are remembered here, where you kept terror away from the homeland for 20 years, and you will be remembered there, whenever freedom howls in the wild winds.

Chapter 1: Shopping Spree!

The midday sun hung high in the sky as Jacob Mooreland's pickup truck sped into the packed parking lot of the super Walmart of Marshall, Arkansas. It was hot and dry this time of year, July of 2028, and it had become normal for the past few years to see a constant large police presence at Walmart, the small town's main shopping venue. The nearby local homeless shelter had steadily grown over the past four years, first to a homeless encampment, and then to a full-blown refugee shantytown in the small city park. Several years ago, this would have been unbelievable, but every small town in America that was within 200 miles of a major city had seen a human wave of desperate and broken city dwellers flee to the rural countryside, where they were at least closer to where the food was grown, and farther from where drug cartels ruled the streets.

The long-time residents of Marshall had done their best to maintain a sense of normalcy, but Jacob knew that, unsurprisingly, they had now surpassed the breaking point. He parked his old Ram 1500 between an empty police car with four slashed tires and an overturned shopping cart, broken eggs and a smashed bottle of pickles spilling out onto the pavement. He looked past the scared, scurrying shoppers and scanned the crazy eyes of drug addicts that were milling around. Jacob visually checked their hands and waistlines.

Who is carrying a weapon and who is feeling froggy today? He double checked his concealed 9mm beneath his jacket. As usual, the tweakers could sense that he was dangerous, and he passed through the doors unmolested.

The atmosphere inside was unusually vile, filled with a palpable tension that seemed to suffocate the aisles. Today was worse than usual. Surprisingly there were no police at the door, and yelling could be heard at the back of one of the food aisles. Cashiers were closing up their drawers quickly and heading for the safe room at the customer service office. Desperation was etched in the faces of the throngs of people who had converged on the store, each driven by the same pressing need for food and basic necessities. The tweakers noticed that something was wrong also, and they began shouting and yelling for joy, heading for the pharmacy and the jewelry aisle. Simultaneously, normal shoppers with shocked faces, looked first at the empty cashier stations, then at the mayhem in the back of the store, and then headed out the doors without paying, looks of guilt and desperation on their faces.

Jacob headed back to the ammo section without hesitating, first grabbing a backpack from the outdoor goods section. Being a survival homesteader, his family's larder had been overflowing for years, but one can never have too much ammo. Fortunately, Walmart had realized that they didn't have sufficient security measures to keep guns any longer, but Jacob arrived to find that a tweaker had already broken the glass door housing the ammunition. "A shipment just arrived for the pharmacy," he told the tweaker, "head on out to the loading docks and get you some. Have fun buddy!"

"Dude you're the best!," replied the tweaker, stumbling off in search of pharmaceuticals, and leaving Jacob to enjoy his ammo shopping spree.

On this day, it was not only the town of Marshall, but inflation had ravaged the entire American economy in recent months, turning into a full-blown depression. It had been triggered by a perfect storm of events: international turmoil, shortages of key resources, disruptions in supply chains, and a government desperately printing money in the form of stimulus checks. Prices had soared, and it felt as though the value of a dollar had dwindled into insignificance.

———————

Despite receiving four hefty stimulus checks in just the past year alone, Americans had watched helplessly as prices continued to rise, relentlessly eroding the purchasing power of not only stimulus money, but of all types of income. The promise of financial relief had turned into a cruel illusion, leaving many struggling to put food on the table and provide for their families. Those on fixed incomes or pensions were destitute overnight, and business owners were all suddenly operating at a loss. Virtually all small businesses closed their doors, and the government was taking unprecedented measures involving direct financial support and use of government assets to keep big box stores operating.

———————

As Jacob navigated the crowded store, from the ammo section back to the exit, he witnessed chaos erupting around him. Police officers had returned to the front doors and were attempting to restore order. Being only a squad of 9 officers, they were overwhelmed by the sheer number of desperate shoppers. Fights began to break out over dwindling supplies, with people clashing viciously for the last remaining cans of beans or bottles of water. The police fired a few warning shots, but the tweakers were taking a new designer drug called "ultraquin," and the warning shots just made them feel like they were at the best carnival ride ever. Ultraquin was made from a cocktail of prescription drugs and users frequently lost most of their hair and were extremely thin, so they tended to all look the same. After realizing that they were outmatched, the police formed a tight perimeter at one of the exits, just to protect themselves, and so the mayhem continued.

Jacob walked quickly to the unblocked door, which quickly was becoming a constricted funnel for the mass of frightened shoppers and excited looters. Directly in front of him and blocking the door, Jacob saw a skinny bald tweaker, wild-eyed and frantic, seize another shopper's cart, sending canned goods and essentials scattering across the floor near the exit. The owner of the cart, a middle-aged woman, confronted the man, her face contorted with rage and desperation. The situation developed rapidly as onlookers watched in horror.

The man spun and jumped, shouting with glee, and then he lunged at the woman like a rabid dog, even letting out a snarl! It was like a scene from a dystopian painting by Hieronymus Bosch, where the demons had been let out from the mouth of the underworld. Jacob pulled his hand from his pocket, gripping a pair of brass knuckles. As he quickly approached, barely looking at the rabid man, Jacob pivoted and in one swift smooth motion, much like a pitcher throwing a baseball, Jacob delivered a crushing blow to the man's temple, sending the tweaker flying into the empty claw crane game, and then straight to the floor, motionless. The woman who had been assaulted seemed frozen. "Times up," Jacob told her, "Get home now!" He knew that he also had to get out of the store before he found himself embroiled in another confrontation, or worse, before he had to hurt someone else to protect his own family's needs. He had as much ammo as he could fit in his backpack, and it was time to move out.

With a sense of urgency gnawing at him, Jacob continued towards his truck, ignoring the drama and desperation around him. Everyone was in need today and there was no saving anyone, except one's self and one's family. He knew he had to make a quick escape from the chaos unfolding in the store. Reaching his vehicle, he hesitated for a moment, gazing back at the Walmart, hoping that some form of order would be restored. But the situation was clearly beyond salvation.

As he sped away from the Walmart parking lot, the feeling of the vicious confrontation he had been part of continued to churn in his mind. He had a family to provide for, and their survival depended on his ability to secure essential supplies without being caught up in the lawlessness that seemed to be consuming the world around them. His destination was clear; he needed to reach the tractor supply store on the other side of town, where he hoped to find a few additional items necessary to sustain his small farm and ensure his family's survival in what would surely be the longest emergency ever, if not the dawn of a new and sinister dark age.

As Jacob drove across town, the weight of the world's recent events bore down on him. His thoughts traveled back in time, tracing the path that had led society to its current dire predicament.

––––––––––

It all began with the conflict in Ukraine, 6 years ago, when the East-West divide became a chasm. The painful and bloody Ukraine war resulted in Russia and its allies withholding and blocking the flow of critical supplies, including natural gas, vital fertilizers, and later petroleum from the middle east. The European Union and the United States had shown resilience, scrambling to make up for the shortages. But that was only the beginning.

Just three years ago, in 2025, the world had witnessed an alarming escalation when China decided it was time to retake Taiwan. The conflict in Taiwan became a protracted war, with the Taiwanese holding out longer than anyone had imagined. The U.S. administration feared getting into a regional conflict, and their aid to Taiwan was indirect and half-hearted, and by 2027, even Taiwanese partisans had been killed or thrown into internment camps for re-education. Starting in 2025 and collaborating with Russia, China also began withholding key supplies from both the European Union and the United States. The trade war repercussions were brutal and shook global markets like never before. Retirement funds based on stock market investments became worthless almost overnight. Back and forth tariffs hurt everyone, but especially American consumers who had grown accustomed to having a world full of products at their fingertips. Fuel prices soared. Fertilizer prices tripled, followed by food, and the ripple effect cascaded through nearly every consumer good until the poor became destitute, the middle class became poor, and the wealthy raised the drawbridges, determined to preserve their status as the United States began i its transformation into a third world economy.

The repercussions were felt most acutely by those already struggling to make ends meet. Poor people were forced to become squatters, and many turned to drugs, their dreams of a better life slipping away. As the cost of living skyrocketed, crime began to spiral out of control, fueled by hopelessness and frustration. By the end of the year 2027, society teetered on the brink of chaos.

Earlier this year, in 2028, a series of alarming events unfolded rapidly. In April, three months prior, Brazil, India, and South Africa had finally followed through on threats to end trade in US dollars, sending shockwaves through the global financial system. The value of the dollar plummeted to unprecedented lows, sinking below even notoriously unstable currencies such as the Argentinian peso. Desperation led the US government to distribute an additional generous round of stimulus checks, intended to quell the flames of discontent among the nation's most vulnerable. Instead, it doubled prices for consumer goods in the United States, deepening the crisis. The U.S. Federal Reserve and Treasury had already raised interest rates to over 25% and had no levers left to pull, the high interest rates only brought lending and business development to a screeching halt, and the value of the dollar did not even bounce after the fall.

Within another month, in May, a third round of stimulus checks followed, largely aimed at preventing the poorest segments of society from erupting into uncontrollable riots. It was bribery, pure and simple, and it too only served to exacerbate inflation, like a vicious cycle that showed no signs of stopping. It was as if the government was saying, "here is another check, please stop rioting." The very fabric of the American economy was unraveling and tearing apart at the seams at an alarming pace.

The final nail in the coffin of the US economy came when the European Union capitulated to the demands of Russia, China, and their allies. They began purchasing petroleum from OPEC in Chinese Yuan and agreed to declare Taiwan a part of China and Ukraine as part of Russia. Overnight, the US economy plummeted into an even worse free fall. Prices doubled once again, and chaos lit up the streets as looters took what they needed. Police in the cities barricaded themselves inside of police stations and formed safe zones in their own police neighborhoods.

A new sort of vigilante, gangland, anarchic order became a grim reality as the divide between the haves and the have-nots became a chasm. Desperate individuals who had already been struggling to put food on the table and pay exorbitant rents, became homeless, some even wandering like refugees. The cities, once symbols of prosperity and opportunity, became entirely inhospitable, their glittering skylines overshadowed by the ever-growing specter of hunger, homelessness, and anarchy, smoke from warming fires hung thick in the city air as tracers zipped across the city skyline from bursts of automatic gunfire throughout the nights.

Normal people quickly began to leave cities in droves. They flocked to smaller and mid-sized communities, their desperation evident as they became homeless on the streets or clustered in makeshift camps of squatters. These camps, initially born out of necessity, soon descended into squalor and lawlessness. Jacob, while driving to town to buy animal feed and trade or sell meat and farm products, bore witness to the unsettling scenes that unfolded in these camps. Desperate individuals resorted to petty crimes to survive, and it became increasingly unsafe to venture into the downtown area of his community. Drug use, robberies, and violence had taken hold, transforming once-thriving neighborhoods into ominous danger zones. Bars were installed on windows and the city government began a program to confiscate foreclosed properties and house police officers and their families that were fleeing from urban areas. These officers then served to increase their own law enforcement numbers, which continued to be insufficient due to the rapidly growing refugee population and the squatter camps that had sprung up in every empty lot and city park.

Amidst this upheaval, some of the newcomers from urban areas sought refuge outside of town, not only in National Forest areas but also on private land, often without permission. These camps sprang up along roadsides, a stark reminder of the fraying social fabric and the exodus taking place out of American cities. Tensions escalated as landowners, many of them struggling themselves, confronted these unwelcome arrivals. In some cases, disputes turned violent, with shots being fired and altercations spiraling out of control. Law enforcement was stretched thin, and more often than not, it was the landowners who found themselves on the wrong side of the law, shipped off to jail while the squatters remained, their makeshift communities growing with each passing day. The once-picturesque landscapes of the American Midwest were marred by these clashes, a testament to the unraveling society in the face of mounting hardships.

For years, long before the crisis reached its current catastrophic state, Jacob had been diligently putting away supplies, drawing on the lessons he'd learned during his many months in third world countries while serving in the United States Army Infantry and Special Operations during GWOT, the Global War on Terrorism. He understood firsthand the harsh realities of struggling to survive in environments where resources were scarce and life's comforts were far from guaranteed. He once felt pride in keeping America safe in the years after 9/11, taking the fight to terrorists overseas so that they couldn't attack the homeland. But more recently, he had seen that Americans were losing faith in their values and were focused on the things that they wanted, rather than who they wanted to be. At the same time, the world was becoming more crowded, countries like China and India were scrambling to find the resources to feed and supply their people. Dictators in other countries like Russia, Brazil, and Iran were happy to act as warlords and despots, profiting from global scarcity.

Jacob had studied history in college and he was a follower of current events in the way that most men follow sports. He knew what was coming and he knew how to prepare. Over the years, he had stockpiled a variety of basic necessities, each one carefully selected based on his experiences in those remote and challenging places. These included staples like dried grains and legumes, canned goods, items for water purification, and a reliable source of renewable energy through solar panels and wind turbines. He also stored away firearms, communications equipment, homestead food production supplies, and sheds full of tools.

As the crisis deepened, Jacob recognized that there were a few critical items he needed to stock up on even more urgently. These items included more ammunition, more salt, more chlorine for water purification, and more seeds. He also sought to amass as much cracked corn feed as possible for his livestock, recognizing that self-sufficiency required tending to their needs. Moreover, he knew that medical supplies were paramount. Antibiotics, even veterinary quality items like penicillin and oxytetracycline, along with wound spray, bandages, syringes, and needles, could mean the difference between life and death in an emergency when access to medical care was uncertain at best.

Entering the Tractor Supply, though still crowded, felt like a relief compared to the chaos of Walmart. Most shoppers had yet to fully grasp the magnitude of the crisis or the long-term implications. They were primarily focused on short-term supplies, grabbing what they needed to get by just for the immediate future. Jacob navigated the aisles, collecting the items he needed.

As he loaded his cart with seeds, salt, antibiotics, and bags of cracked corn feed, Jacob focused on his task at hand. He knew that the items he was accumulating were not mere luxuries but necessities for survival. In a world where industrial supply chains were breaking down; the availability of these critical supplies would become increasingly scarce. Items like ammunition for hunting and self-defense, seeds for long-term self-sufficient agriculture, and knowledge of basic survival skills would be invaluable assets in the uncertain years to come. Jacob understood that his journey towards self-sufficiency was far from over, and the road ahead would require every ounce of resourcefulness, knowledge, and determination he possessed.

Jacob made his way to the cash register, his cart laden with the crucial supplies he had gathered for his family's survival. The line was long and sluggish, stretching through the store as shoppers jostled and grumbled, their impatience mounting. As he inched closer to the cashier, he overheard snippets of discontent from the shoppers behind him, their frustration palpable.

Finally, it was his turn. The cashier, her face etched with nervous tension, demanded, "Cash only! Prices are four times what they were last week. You understand, right?"

Jacob met her gaze with unwavering confidence. He had anticipated this, and though it seemed surreal to be paying four times the amount he had just a week earlier, he had cash on hand. "I understand," he replied calmly, placing the items on the counter.

The cashier's fingers trembled slightly as she rang up the purchases, her eyes darting between the items and the cash. "It's going to be $4350 in cash," she said, her voice wavering.

Jacob counted out 44 one hundred dollar bills methodically, handing over the cash without hesitation. "Here you go. Keep the change." He knew it would be worthless in 24 hours anyway.

As the transaction concluded, a chorus of impatient shoppers behind Jacob grew louder. "Hoarder!" one person muttered. Another grumbled, "This is ridiculous. What about doing things for 'the Greater Good'." Jacob was beginning to hear this slogan everywhere, 'the Greater Good.' From what he had gathered, it was a way to make people feel guilty for being self-reliant, as if society was collapsing from self-reliance, rather than from drug use, overstretched supply lines, and global financial failures.

Jacob, unfazed by the muttered comments, pushed his heavy cart towards the exit. He understood the frustration of those in line but knew that his determination to secure supplies for his family was worth it. In this emerging dystopian world, survival required adaptability, resourcefulness, and the ability to navigate the chaos of the present while keeping an eye on the uncertain future.

Jacob hurried towards his truck, a sense of urgency tugging at him as muscled the heavy cart forward. But as he reached his vehicle, dread washed over him. The passenger side window had been shattered, and a stranger was frantically going through his belongings, a bald tweaker with his face twisted by desperation. Jacob's pulse quickened, and adrenaline surged through his veins as he realized the imminent danger.

Without hesitation, Jacob's military training kicked in. He had carried his nine-millimeter concealed in a holster on his left side, a precaution he had hoped he would never need to take. In one fluid motion, he reached across his chest from right to left, unsnapping and removing the weapon, aiming it at the man.

"Get out!," Jacob shouted, his voice commanding authority. "Get away from my truck!"

The criminal, a man whose eyes were filled with an insane, rabid glee, responded defiantly, fueled by a cocktail of drugs and desperation. "You think you can tell me what to do?" he snarled, dropping Jacob's ammo boxes.

Their voices clashed in a tense standoff, each word dripping with aggression. The criminal's hand darted into the backseat of Jacob's truck, fingers closing around a crowbar. With a menacing grin, he advanced, ready to strike.

Time seemed to stretch agonizingly as Jacob faced a life-altering decision. The adrenaline coursed through his veins, heart pounding in his chest. He knew he had to act to protect himself. "You ain't got it in ya', sheep, sheep!," said the tweaker.

"Wrong answer," Jacob replied, and squeezed the trigger twice, the sharp reports echoing in the air.

The criminal fell away from the truck and crumpled to the ground, a look of shock and pain contorting his face. He struggled to breathe, gasping for air as his life drained away before finally managing one last drug-induced smile, blood trickling out of the corner of his mouth; and then stillness. It was a chilling sight, one that Jacob knew he would carry with him forever. Being a combat veteran, the feeling wasn't entirely new. The adrenaline high was like heroin, but seeing the bright red blood spill out onto the pavement was like watching the blue fade from the sky for the last time, knowing that you were responsible. Jacob knew what to do, he silently nodded over his shoulder toward the invisible darkness of the grim reaper that had followed him for years ever since his first kill, and whispered, "Better luck next time."

Shaking off the moment, a strange mix of emotions coursed through him as he approached his truck once more. Adrenaline and excitement mingled with a chilling realization of what he had just done. His fingertips barely registered the sensation of the steering wheel as he started the engine and drove away, feeling as if he was floating above the pavement due to the adrenaline high, leaving behind the scene of the desperate confrontation.

Chapter 2: Remembering the Leap Off Grid

Ten years prior, Jacob stood at the crossroads of his military career. He had spent the last decade serving his country, deploying to numerous foreign lands, and witnessing the world change in ways that left him increasingly disenchanted. As he prepared to retire from the military, his thoughts were consumed by the state of the nation and the world. He found himself questioning the path his beloved country was on.

He remembered a mild evening in their quaint suburban home, and Jacob sat on the porch, gazing out at the setting sun. Ana, his young Croatian wife, joined him, her presence a source of strength and solace in uncertain times.

"Can you believe it's been five years since we were married?" Ana mused, her fingers gently tracing the contours of a photo on her phone, as if she could touch the past. It was a picture of their wedding day, captured in a moment of pure joy.

Jacob turned to her, his eyes filled with warmth. "Time has a way of slipping through our fingers, doesn't it?"

She smiled, her deep blue eyes reflecting the fading sun. "It's been quite a journey, hasn't it, Jacob?"

He nodded, a hint of seriousness clouding his features. "Indeed, Ana. I can't help but wonder about the world we're creating for our children."

The world outside their comfortable home was changing rapidly. Economic disparity and moral decay was growing, and a sense of disillusionment had settled upon Jacob. His years of military service had taken him to remote corners of the globe, where he'd witnessed firsthand the consequences of corruption, bureaucracy, and failed governance. It left him with a lingering unease about the state of his own country.

"The things I've seen out there, Ana, and I know you have too, especially when you were growing up," Jacob began, his voice tinged with a mix of frustration and sadness, "it's as if we're headed down the same path where other failed countries have gone. We're supposed to be a beacon of hope and freedom, ambition and morality, but it's starting to feel like we're losing our way as a country."

Ana leaned in closer, her hand finding his. "You've always had a strong sense of duty and self-reliance, Jacob. It's one of the things I admire most about you."

He appreciated her support, but the weight of his concerns pressed heavily upon him. "I thought serving in the military would make a difference, but sometimes I wonder if we're just pawns in a larger game. The world's problems seem insurmountable."

Ana squeezed his hand reassuringly. "But you've made a difference in the lives you've touched; in the missions you've carried out. You've brought hope to many, even if you can't change the world all by yourself."

Jacob sighed, acknowledging the truth in her words. "You're right, Ana. Maybe I just need some time to figure out where we fit into all of this. I think it is time for me to start focusing on what we can do ourselves; how we can rely on ourselves more. I'd like to build something myself, grow things, make our own little piece of the world flourish."

As the sun dipped below the horizon, the couple continued to talk, sharing their hopes and dreams for the future, not knowing that a decade later, they would face a world transformed by unforeseen challenges and uncertainties.

In the weeks following that first conversation, and with the weight of their conversation about the state of the world still fresh in their minds, Jacob and Ana continued to explore the idea of finding a place where they could live life on their own terms, away from the complexities and uncertainties of the modern world.

"I've been doing some research," Jacob began, his voice filled with anticipation, "and I think I've found the perfect place for us, Ana. It's a remote property in the Ozark Mountains of Arkansas, far from the chaos of city life. It's got everything we need to be self-sufficient: fresh water, fertile soil, 100 acres of hunting land, and complete privacy."

Ana's eyes sparkled with interest. She had always been an adventurer at heart, and missed the remote Croatian mountains of her childhood. The idea of starting anew in the serene mountains was exhilarating. "Tell me more about it," she urged.

Jacob retrieved a folder from the nearby table and began laying out maps and photographs. "It's about 100 acres of pristine wilderness, untouched by development. The property sits on a hill, offering breathtaking views of the surrounding landscape. There's a clear, bubbling stream that runs through it, providing us with all the fresh water we'll ever need."

Ana's gaze drifted over the images, imagining the possibilities. "It sounds like a dream come true."

"It gets better," Jacob continued, his excitement growing. "The soil is rich and fertile, perfect for growing our own food. We'll have complete control over what we eat, and we can sustain ourselves year-round."

As Ana listened to her husband's vision, she could feel her heart pounding with anticipation. "And what about shelter?"

Jacob smiled and pointed to a photograph of a picturesque clearing. "There's a perfect spot for our homestead. We can build a cabin from the timber on the property, using sustainable and energy-efficient designs. Off the grid, self-sufficient. Or if you are up for the challenge we could build something more robust, maybe out of concrete. Have you ever seen an Earth-sheltered home? They are easy to heat and cool because they have a roof and three sides underground. The fourth side faces the south, letting sunlight in during wintertime to keep it bright and warm."

Ana leaned in closer, her enthusiasm matching Jacob's. "I like the idea of a home like that, I bet it's cozy. And you know how my dad makes fun of Americans for building all of their big fancy homes out of sticks. He would love that. It sounds like the life we've always talked about."

"It does, doesn't it?" Jacob agreed. "We'll be able to teach the kids about self-reliance, hard work, and the importance of nature. It's a chance to live authentically, and close to God's creation."

Ana nodded, her heart full of excitement. "Let's go take a look at it, Jacob. Let's see if it's as perfect as it sounds."

The couple embarked on a journey to visit the remote property in the Ozark Mountains that held the promise of a new beginning. As they walked through the pristine wilderness, their laughter and shared dreams filled the air, creating a sense of anticipation for the life they were about to build together.

They started their exploration at the top of a hill, from which they could see the entirety of their property. The rolling hills and lush forests stretched all the way down to the year-round creek, with only one entrance and forest on all sides of the property, painting a picture of serenity and seclusion. The nearest paved road was four miles away and the whole property was surrounded by National Forest.

Jacob pointed to the clear, babbling stream that meandered through the land. "Look at that, Ana. Fresh water right at our doorstep, and the realtor says that most wells in the area aren't deeper than 50 feet, shallow enough for a hand pump."

Ana nodded, her eyes tracing the course of the stream. "Perfect for irrigation and providing us with emergency drinking water."

As they ventured further into the property, they discovered an abundance of wildlife. Deer grazed peacefully in the open meadows, while the forest was alive with the sounds of birdsong. The land was teeming with potential for hunting and foraging.

"Game is plentiful here," Jacob observed. "We won't have to worry about going hungry. Lots of white oak trees mean acorns for deer and yet another emergency food source." He truly was a survivalist at heart and his mind was prepping 24-7.

Their exploration led them to a particularly picturesque clearing surrounded by towering hardwood trees. It had a gentle, south-facing slope, and a commanding view of the property. Much of the back side dropped off towards a steep cliff so it would be difficult to approach from the rear. Jacob could hardly contain his excitement as he gestured to the spot. "This is where we can build our cabin, Ana. Right here."

Ana stood in the clearing, taking in the tranquil surroundings. "It's perfect, Jacob. We'll have a front-row seat to nature every day". Their love had always been strong, but being in that clearing together on that day, their love became a force of nature, and their embrace was deeper than earthly passion."

Over the next several weeks, they spent countless hours planning and envisioning the layout of their future homestead, sketching rough plans on paper, and discussing the details of their earth-sheltered home. A solar panel array, rainwater collection, and raised bed gardens all became part of their vision for a sustainable and self-reliant lifestyle.

"Finding that property is a dream come true," Ana murmured, her eyes shining with hope. "It's also near Bullard Air Force Base, where my sister lives. We will be close to family!" Ana's sister Mia was married to an Air Force Pilot named Mark Rinehart and Mia was the only family she had in the United States.

Jacob couldn't have agreed more. "And we'll do it all together, Ana. Building our home, teaching the kids about self-sufficiency, and embracing the simple life."

The couple shared a moment of quiet reflection before Ana turned to Jacob with a mischievous grin. "But what should we name our homestead?"

Jacob chuckled, delighted by his wife's enthusiasm. "How about 'Blue Spring Farm'?"

Ana's eyes lit up with approval. "I love it. 'Blue Spring' it is."

With their homestead officially named and plans in motion, they went back to close the deal and explore the property, mentally marking spots for gardens, a barn, and other structures. As they walked hand in hand through the lush landscape, their shared vision for the future solidified, and their excitement for the journey ahead grew stronger with each step.

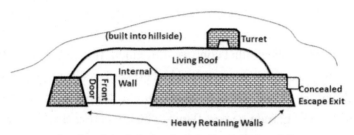

Jacob and Ana's design for their Earth Sheltered Home

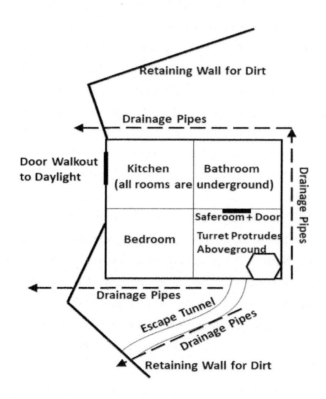

Jacob and Ana's Floor Layout for their Earth-Sheltered Home

25

Chapter 3: Back to Blue Spring

Jacob hit the gas pedal hard, his truck racing through the streets of the chaotic town. The thought of getting pulled over by the police didn't concern him much; they were all tied up trying to control the riots that had erupted. As he passed the Walmart, a plume of thick black smoke billowed from the outdoor and garden center, flames already eating through the roof. The police could still be seen 'strong pointing' one entrance, but people were still streaming in and out through the other exit, their desperation palpable. Some were thieves, others were just going after food.

Further down the road, a full-blown riot was in progress at the Aldi, with enraged individuals clashing with only 3 or 4 police officers. Objects were being hurled through the air, and angry shouts filled the streets. The scene was one of chaos and lawlessness, and Jacob knew he had to keep moving to get back to his homestead and his family. He was beginning to doubt his judgment for deciding to go on one last supply run.

As he sped past the riot, he encountered reckless drivers on the road, all vying to escape the turmoil gripping the town. Some cars careened dangerously; their occupants equally desperate to leave. Jacob navigated the treacherous road carefully, his instincts honed by years of driving military vehicles in chaotic combat zones. He knew that the key was to pay attention to detail, and keep an eye out for danger not only directly in front of you, but also far up the road.

Stay Frosty Jacob, continue to scan, near, medium, far, near, medium, far, both sides, up and down, head on a swivel...

It was a tense and harrowing journey, a microcosm of the world spiraling into chaos, but he was determined to reach his family and the safety of their off-grid homestead in the Arkansas Ozark Mountains, just 20 miles away.

As Jacob continued on his journey, he rounded a curve and approached one of the town's makeshift homeless camps that was sprawled haphazardly along the roadside near what was once a playground and park. The scene was one of disorder and disarray, a stark contrast to the natural beauty that had once defined the area. For months now, since the economic crisis had intensified, this camp had grown messier by the day. Tents were pitched at odd angles, and garbage was strewn about like a twisted mosaic of desperation. It was a testament to the times, a place where people had been forced to seek refuge when all else had crumbled.

———

The park where the camp had taken root was a stark reflection of the world's transformation. Once a pristine and beautiful space, it had been a place where children used to play freely and families had gathered for joyous occasions like the annual Fourth of July fair. But now, the park was a shadow of its former self, marred by the encampment and the signs of struggle that had taken hold. The laughter of children and the festivities of the past seemed like distant memories.

As Jacob drove past, a heavy sense of nostalgia washed over him. He knew that the good times in the park, like the once-thriving economy, were relics of the past. The world had changed irreversibly, and the future held uncertainty and challenges that he couldn't yet fathom. The park, once a symbol of community and happiness, now stood as a solemn reminder of the world they had lost, a world that might never return.

———————

As Jacob rounded the second corner beside the park, he was met with an unexpected and unsettling sight. Lawless occupants of the area had taken it upon themselves to set up a makeshift checkpoint, spilling across the road like a flowing garbage dump. It was obvious to Jacob, a veteran who had seen proper military checkpoints during his service, that this one was no official checkpoint, but more like a 'troll under the bridge' location to steal your belonging and maybe kill you.

The makeshift checkpoint consisted of a couple of vehicles and burning tires, haphazardly blocking most of the road. It was clearly hastily thrown up, random, and confusing, manned by several tweakers and likely some ex-convicts. Several wrecked cars lay strewn about the area, their shattered windows and twisted metal bearing witness to the chaos that had unfolded. Stolen goods were scattered across the ground, testaments to the lawlessness and thefts that had occurred thus far.

Even more unsettling were three lifeless bodies that lay beside the road, grim reminders of the violence that had permeated the camp. More innocent people, their faces etched with fear and despair, were currently being held up by the criminals. Some were crying as their vehicles were ransacked, their possessions callously plundered. It was a nightmarish tableau, a stark illustration of the cruelty that could emerge when society unraveled, and desperation ruled the day. Jacob knew he had to navigate this treacherous terrain with caution and a steely resolve to protect himself and to reach his family.

As Jacob's mindset shifted from peaceful survival mode to combat mode, his heart raced with a rush of memories from his deployments in the Middle East. Another spike of adrenaline coursed through his veins, awakening instincts that had lain dormant for years before today. He let up on the gas pedal and slowed his vehicle, feigning compliance as he approached the makeshift checkpoint. His combat-honed senses were still razor sharp, and in that crucial moment, he made his move.

Let's do this. What you got boys? With a sudden surge of adrenaline sending a tingling sensation from the base of his spine to the top of his skull, Jacob swerved his truck sharply to the right towards two of the criminals. With rifles slung over their shoulders they had been flagging him down, but they were caught off guard by this unexpected maneuver, leaping off the roadway to escape. He felt a grim satisfaction as he simultaneously aimed his nine-millimeter pistol out the left driver's side window, firing two rapid shots at the face of a third criminal, landing only the first shot which snapped the man's bald head sharply backward as he suddenly straightened upward like a board and then toppled sideways to the ground. In a split second, Jacob's truck was speeding off as he ran down a fourth, less alert tweaker under the middle of his vehicle, with two dull thuds. Jacob didn't look back.

He had quickly cleared the makeshift checkpoint, exhilaration coursing through him like a potent drug. It was a sensation that before today, he hadn't felt since his time in the military, and it gripped him with a force he couldn't deny. It was a high, an addiction rekindled, and he knew he had to fight the urge to indulge further.

But even as he pressed on, several of the criminals who hadn't been paying attention began to fire wildly at his truck from a growing distance, a single round shattering the back window. The temptation to execute a U-turn and confront the remaining threats was strong, but a sobering realization hit him like a punch to the gut. His family depended on him to bring back supplies, and getting caught up in further violence was not the path he needed to take. Jacob took a deep breath, his grip on the steering wheel steady.

"Calm down," he muttered to himself, *his voice a soothing counterpoint to the chaos of the moment. "Focus on what's important. Get home to Ana and the kids."* He pushed aside the adrenaline-fueled excitement, reminding himself of the responsibility he carried, and drove south towards his family and their uncertain future.

As Jacob left the chaos of the town behind, the countryside gradually began to resemble normalcy and peace, as if the tumultuous events in the town were worlds away. He felt for a moment, almost like a fugitive from justice after having killed or injured at least 6 men, but then reminded himself that law and order was gone, and the laws of combat now applied. His thoughts drifted back to the years of preparation he had dedicated to safeguarding his family against the looming specter of a doomsday scenario or disaster.

It all began years ago, during his deployments in Third World countries with the military, Jacob had witnessed the stark realities of poverty and social unrest. Those experiences had left an indelible mark on him, teaching him invaluable lessons about the fragility of society. He understood that the threads holding civilization together were far more delicate than most people realized, and when even just a few of those threads unraveled, suffering multiplied exponentially.

In those distant lands, in Africa, Latin America, the Balkans, and the Middle East, he had seen people who battled hunger almost daily, their gaunt faces a testament to the scarcity of food. Many suffered from dysentery and diarrhea due to contaminated water sources, and the struggle for clean drinking water was a constant one. People scavenged for scraps of plastic and cardboard to patch up their makeshift homes, and a scrap of tin roof was considered a precious treasure, a symbol of hope amid hardship.

The memories of those experiences were etched into Jacob's consciousness. They had shaped his understanding of what it meant to be prepared, to be self-reliant, and to ensure the well-being of his family in an uncertain world. The dedication to those lessons had driven him to stockpile supplies, develop survival skills, and establish an off-grid homestead in the Arkansas Ozark Mountains. Now, as he navigated the peaceful countryside, he knew that his preparations were more crucial than ever, for the thin threads that held society together were fraying, and the future remained uncertain.

After returning from the military, Jacob's deepest yearning was to live in a peaceful, rural area where he could raise a family on a small farm or homestead. He envisioned a life tending to cattle and goats, harvesting hay from the fields, and instilling in his children the values of hard work and strong moral character that he had learned growing up on a farm when he was a boy.

In his eyes, growing up on a farm was not just about sustenance but about nurturing a sense of responsibility and resilience in children. It taught them the value of hard work, the importance of caring for animals, and the satisfaction of providing for their family through their own efforts. It also taught children about hard limits, how to deal with death, and how to work through pain and cold. If you leave the faucet running, you can actually run out of water. Livestock dies and you have to at least cope with that sort of death. It's winter and too cold to feed your animals and do chores? Too bad! You are too sick to do farm work? Too bad, you have to be tough and pragmatic on a farm.

Despite having created a good life for their children in a fairly affluent country and a welcoming community, Jacob could never quite shake the awareness that the world had the potential to turn difficult. That unease had driven him to build a fortified home for his family, similar to a bunker; an earth-sheltered home. This was proving to have been a wise decision, because of its clear durability during natural disasters and its energy efficiency in heating and cooling in a grid down situation.

Within their home, he had constructed a secure safe room, a sanctuary to protect their loved ones from the unpredictable elements of criminal activity or natural disasters. The peace of mind that came with having a refuge was immeasurable.

Together with his wife, they had diligently stockpiled food supplies and other essentials, always preparing for unforeseen circumstances. While many were focused on securing only the very basic necessities, Jacob and his wife understood the importance of longer-term staples like salt, animal feed, and essential building and maintenance supplies. In the event of a societal collapse, they had enough salt and water-purifying chlorine that they would even be able to trade these crucial items with neighbors.

At times, doubt had crept into his mind, causing him to question the financial investments made in preparation for disasters that might never occur. But now, as unease settled over the world, he felt a quiet vindication that their preparations had placed them in a better position than most.

———————

As he continued his journey south on the curvy two lane state highway, highway 77, Jacob was still lost deep in his thoughts. *I've seen tough times before, and we'll get through this one too. A brief, heartfelt prayer to the Lord for strength and guidance gave him the resolve to press on, no matter the challenges that lay ahead.*

He had made a promise to God long ago that if he could survive the war then he would take his family to a quiet corner of the Earth to build, grow, and create in honor of the Creator, and to give thanks for the mercy that had allowed him to survive when many of his friends had not. They had spent years under the dirt now, some in Arlington, others around the country. Meanwhile, his life had been allowed to continue, and he tried every day to honor the sacrifice of the fallen, as flawed and imperfect as his efforts were. In any case, he was determined to give a good accounting of himself as he faced the modern horrors that were unfolding on this day.

Turning onto his familiar dirt road, Jacob couldn't help but marvel at the breathtaking beauty that surrounded him. The narrow road ran alongside a crystal-clear river, its waters shimmering in the rays of sunlight that filtered through the lush canopy of trees. Birds chirped melodiously, and the gentle rustling of leaves provided a soothing soundtrack to his journey. It was a place of serenity and solace, a refuge from the troubles of the world. Despite the tranquility, a defensive plan was always needed according to a military veteran like Jacob, ALWAYS.

Just one quarter mile after turning off of Highway 77, Jacob passed a small white farmhouse owned by Jeb and Laura Roberts. They were a religious family, easy to get along with, but not very social. They lived in an exposed spot, right on the small county road. Long ago, Jacob had arranged with Jeb and the other neighbors to drop trees and blockade the road if the situation with the outside world destabilized enough. It was time to execute that plan, but first, he had to get home. He sped past Jeb's and on down the road.

Suddenly, about a mile further down, the tranquil scene was shattered as Jacob rounded a bend and came face to face with a grim obstacle. An old, gutted and broken down RV camper had been haphazardly laid out across the road, effectively blocking his path. Steep hills rose up on one side and the river was on the other, he was in a fatal funnel and there was no way around. His heart sank as he caught sight of the occupants, a motley crew of 5 or 6 dirty and disheveled individuals armed with an assortment of weapons, mostly hunting rifles, all of them bald from their use of the drug, ultraquin. Desperation coursed through him, a pit formed in his stomach; he was still two miles from home and his vehicle was loaded with vital supplies for his family. Now he faced a treacherous standoff with these menacing drug addict criminals.

No matter, time to Ranger up... He quickly measured how to navigate this unexpected obstacle and bust through to the other side. With adrenaline still surging from events earlier in the day, Jacob made a split-second decision. Gripping the steering wheel tightly, he slammed his foot on the gas pedal, aiming for the rear of the RV, which was the lighter end of the vehicle. He ducked low behind the dash of his vehicle, using the sturdy engine block as a makeshift shield to protect himself from the hail of bullets that began to ping off the hood and smash through the windshield. The powerful Cummins engine of his truck roared to life as he accelerated, the thrill of the moment washing over him. The impact was jarring as his truck rammed into the RV, smacking his jaw on the steering wheel, and spinning the RV violently while sending the truck careening 30 feet past, only to skid to a stop in the ditch.

Chaos erupted as the four heavily armed defenders around the RV fired wildly at him. As the world outside his windshield blurred in a dizzying whirlwind, Jacob's heart raced with exhilaration. The metallic screech of the collision still echoed in his ears, and the sensation of being in the eye of a storm filled him with both dread and determination. With the taste of blood in his mouth, he stayed low and hit the gas while jerking the steering wheel back onto the road.

The deafening noise of gunfire and the rattling of the vehicle punctuated the air. More bullets punctured the metal exterior of Jacob's truck, sending fragments of glass and debris flying as he muscled the steering wheel and got the truck back up on the gravel and moving once again in the right direction. The intense danger of the situation became palpable as the tweakers' checkpoint faded in the rearview mirror, and Jacob knew that he had narrowly escaped a life-threatening situation. The adrenaline-fueled rush was undeniable.

Relief and disbelief surged through Jacob as he sped away from the violent encounter at the makeshift checkpoint. The world outside his windshield now appeared serene, and for a fleeting moment, he felt a sense of invincibility that he hadn't experienced since his days as a young, enlisted man deployed overseas. The rush of surviving a harrowing ordeal flooded his senses, and he couldn't help but mutter to himself about his incredible luck, a trait that had seemed to follow him throughout his life. *Fortune's favorite, his father used to tell him, boy, you are Fortune's favorite!* He pounded the dashboard shouting, "Yeah, good girl!"

As his excitement began to wane, a sudden chill gripped his heart. He glanced down at his side, where he had felt an unusual warmth spreading. At first, he thought it was hot water, but the realization hit him like a lightning bolt—it was blood. A bullet had grazed him, passing between the meat of his pectoral muscle and the skin of his armpit. A lucky miss, a near-miss that left him both shaken and grateful.

Damn, I've always been lucky but... His thoughts expressed a quiet acknowledgment of the many close calls he had faced in his life. The thought of how easily his luck could have run out hung heavy in the air, and he knew he needed to remain vigilant.

But then, panic clawed its way back into his consciousness as his vehicle unexpectedly began to sputter and die. His heart raced as he struggled to pump the gas, but it was no use.

No, no, s@$&! With a final, desperate cough, the engine ceased, leaving him stranded on the road, so close, but not close enough to home. He was about 1 mile past the RV but still 2 miles away from home.

His mind raced through the possibilities of what could have caused the sudden breakdown, but it wasn't until he caught a faint whiff of gasoline that the truth became clear. A bullet had punctured the fuel tank, and the precious fuel had leaked out, leaving him stranded and vulnerable. At least it hadn't caught fire; lucky again.

With his vehicle now a silent testament to his predicament, Jacob realized that he was still far from home, and the weight of his situation pressed upon him like an insurmountable burden. He had enough supplies to make several trips on foot, but the daunting journey that lay ahead, coupled with the ever-present danger of the bandits behind him, filled him with a sense of both dread and determination.

As Jacob surveyed the supplies he had painstakingly gathered from the store, his mind raced through a mental checklist. The situation was dire, and he knew he couldn't carry everything. He had to make calculated decisions about what to leave behind.

Grudgingly, he eliminated the heavier items from his list—bulky sacks of salt and cracked corn feed were deemed impractical for the steep climb through the hills that lay ahead. Instead, he opted for a more strategic selection: seeds for planting, ammunition, and some antibiotics. These items were essential for the survival of his family, their value far outweighing their weight. Luckily, he still had the backpack to carry them in.

His thoughts turned to the criminals on the road, the menacing figures he had left behind. He was fairly confident the rickety RV was out of commission, and he knew they couldn't follow him on foot very quickly, but the sinking sun cast long shadows, and he suspected that if they could figure out where he lived, they might arrive at his home by nightfall. He wasn't sure but he thought one of the tweakers looked like Lester Cutshall, from a family of criminals and thieves that lived 10 miles further down the county road. It was always hard to tell one tweaker from the next once they had been taking ultraquin for a few months, with their bald heads, gaunt cheeks, and hunched frames. Time was not on his side, and he needed to reach the safety of his off-grid homestead before his pursuers closed in.

With his chosen supplies secured in the backpack and an additional makeshift "buttpack" crafted from a seat cover folded over his belt and secured around his hips, Jacob embarked on his journey, immediately leaving the rocky roadway, and traversing rough and unforgiving terrain on foot.

The path home was not a straightforward one, and he found himself scaling hills, scrambling up steep rocky cliffs, and navigating dense forests that seemed to conspire against his progress. Each step was a physical and mental challenge, the weight of his responsibility as well as the supplies bearing down on him.

As he moved with determination, the rugged terrain tested his endurance, his muscles burning with exertion. He pressed on, guided by the knowledge that his family's well-being depended on his ability to reach them in time. Every obstacle, every steep incline, and every thorny thicket he encountered was a reminder of the lengths he would go to protect those he loved. He was careful to cover his tracks and not leave any sign of his passing.

Jacob's heart swelled with relief and a sense of homecoming as he finally spotted his cherished refuge through the thick forest. Quietly, he made his way down a familiar path, his footsteps soft against the earth. The journey had been grueling, but the sight of his off-grid homestead, dubbed "Blue Spring," in the Arkansas Ozark Mountains, filled him with a profound sense of accomplishment and hope.

———

Along the way, he couldn't help but reminisce about the incredible journey that he and his wife had undertaken to build their earth-sheltered home years ago. The memories flooded back, each one a testament to their excellent foresight that motivated them to prepare for the possibility of surviving in this very place during difficult times such as these.

His fondest recollections of the first years there centered on the eldest two children, Jacob, and Emma, who had played amidst the chaos of home construction. They kept themselves entertained with stuffed animals, pretending to be horses or dogs. Those carefree moments of the children were a stark contrast to the tireless work he and his wife had poured into the home's construction. Struggle and joy, side by side, all rolled into one joyous life together. Their shared vision had been clear: to create a sanctuary that would stand as a bastion of safety and self-sufficiency.

Together, they had meticulously planned every detail, from sourcing water to raising their own food. Rainwater harvesting systems, gardens, and livestock pens were all part of their self-reliance strategy. They even saved up enough money to drill a well on their hilltop and then buy a water-pumping windmill. About 15 miles down highway 77, past his own county road, there was a community of Amish that Jacob had hired to erect and install the windmill, as well as pour a concrete water tank higher up the hill above the house. This gave the family a clean, year-round, gravity fed water source. Jacob frequently visited these Amish for off-grid inspiration, and to hire them to help on his homestead. He hoped that they would weather the storm of chaos and be prepared to defend themselves as society collapsed all around them.

The Mooreland family's preparations extended beyond the physical aspects of their homestead. Jacob and his wife had dedicated countless hours to devising security measures, should the need ever arise to defend their home and loved ones. They had hoped that these measures would never be put to the test, but now, with uncertainty looming, their meticulous planning was about to face its most significant trial.

Jacob's thoughts were filled with gratitude for the lessons they had learned, the hard work they had invested, and the resilience they had cultivated together as a family as he traversed the hills leading back to his family and homestead.

He knew that Ana and the children would be hunkered down in the safe room while they awaited his return. Cellphone service was out as part of the new normal and he had foolishly left his GMRS "walkie talkie" at home during this trip.

Chapter 4: Fox in the Hen house

About 100 yards away from his home, Jacob could hear that the family dog, Max, a 150 lb. Anatolian shepherd, began barking uncontrollably. Max was inside a livestock fence alongside the house, and he respected fences. If there were intruders, then he would likely not bite them, but he would not stop barking until his owners acknowledged his alert. Jacob dropped his supplies, armed with only his 9mm pistol, and he picked up the pace, jogging towards his home. Who was the dog barking at, was he barking at Jacob? Or someone else? Jacob's heart skipped a beat as he came to an abrupt halt, grateful for his instinctual silence. The setting sun was now casting long shadows across the tree-filled homestead and grassy meadows. The goat barn stood on the hill to the left and straight ahead stood the wooden shop that Jacob and Ana had painstakingly built by hand, nestled a mere 100 feet before the entrance to his home. His ears strained to pick up the faint sounds of rustling and movement within the shop, despite the dog barking behind the fence further down the hill. Just then, through the door's partial opening, he could glimpse someone rummaging through his tool drawer, greedily filling a bag with his hard-earned possessions and valuable hand tools.

Cautiously, he shifted behind a nearby tree, the rough bark scratching at his palms. Within moments, the intruder's face came into focus, illuminated by a sliver of sunlight filtering into the shop. It was Jesse Cutshall, a notorious petty thief and drug addict who had spent years in and out of jail. He was also the younger brother to the tweaker that Jacob thought he saw near the RV on the county road.

————————

The Cutshall family was considered by many to be emblematic of poverty-stricken white trash, though their hardships were as much a result of their own mental challenges, possibly stemming from inbreeding or environmental factors, such as tainted water or unhealthy diets, as well as from drug abuse. They had gone through the entire evolution of drug habits, from pot, to crack, to meth, to opioids, fentanyl, and now to ultraquin. Drug dealers and manufacturers loved ultraquin because it was a cold brew process, and there was no risk of explosion during manufacture. Jacob could tell now that Jesse had been on the drug, as his hair was completely gone.

————————

As Jacob observed Jesse's frenzied actions, he couldn't help but wonder about the whereabouts of Jesse's older brother, Lester, who was even more of a hardened criminal and had a history of violence. An unsettling memory resurfaced, one from a few years back when Lester had brutally beaten a fellow high school student until the victim had been left hospitalized with a traumatic brain injury. The entire community had seen the beating on circulating social media. Despite this evidence, the leniency of Lester's punishment in that case still haunted Jacob, just two years in juvenile detention; it was a stark reminder of the failures of the justice system. Jesse was more of a sneaky thief and quieter than his older brother, a devious dimwit.

In the quiet dim light, as the sun faded behind low clouds, Jacob's thoughts raced. He knew that his family was safely locked in the safe room, so he put that worry out of his mind. Over the years, he had meticulously planned for a scenario where law enforcement proved incapable of keeping their neighborhood safe from the Cutshall family. It was a scenario he had hoped never to confront but for which he had always felt compelled to prepare.

In hushed conversations with his fellow neighbors, Jacob had delved into increasingly dire scenarios, knowing that preparedness sometimes meant confronting unthinkable possibilities. The talks had strayed into darker territory, where some proposed more extreme measures for dealing with Jesse and Lester Cutshall, young men whose criminality seemed beyond redemption. No one could reason with those two brothers.

Among the whispered discussions were unsettling notions of taking matters into their own hands, of resorting to violence to rid their community of this menace. Some spoke of ambushes, of waiting in the shadows with firearms, ready to confront the Cutshall brothers with lethal force. Others contemplated staging accidents—fires that would consume their ramshackle home, or vehicular mishaps that could plausibly appear as accidents. The aim was clear: to remove the threat posed by Jesse and Lester once and for all.

Unspoken but understood among this close-knit group of neighbors was the grim reality that if these plans ever materialized, they had already identified remote locations deep in the forest, where shallow graves had been dug. The land had instead only become a repository of their collective desperation, a place where they hoped the darkest contingency would never need to be fulfilled. It was a testament to the gravity of their situation and the lengths to which they were willing to go to protect their families and the fragile peace that they had cultivated in their corner of the Ozark Mountains.

―――――――

As Jacob watched Jesse Cutshall pilfering his treasured shop, he knew he faced a difficult decision. Confronting the intruder was tempting, but the safety of his family took precedence over all else. It was a precarious situation, one where a single petty thief posed a threat that couldn't be underestimated, yet Jacob understood that his responsibility as a husband and father far outweighed the desire for retribution.

Carefully, he navigated a little closer through the trees, skirting around the wooden shop where Jesse was busy snooping, moving behind a thicket between the shop and his home. The security measures he had meticulously installed over the years came into play—locked metal yard gates, sturdy fences, and a reinforced code entry door lock. These measures had been put in place not just to keep outsiders at bay but to safeguard his family from the unforeseen dangers that could arise in these troubled times.

With a practiced hand, Jacob silently entered his home, ensuring that all entrances were securely locked behind him. His objective was clear: reach the basement, where the safe room offered a haven of security. Cell phone signals had been down all day, leaving no means of communication with his family other than face-to-face interaction. He left Jesse momentarily in the shop and being the skilled Army Ranger that he was, Jacob slipped unnoticed, to the cupola above the underground home.

With a deep breath, he unlocked the steel trap door and descended the stairs, and then approached the heavily fortified safe room door. The stakes were high, and he knew that the safety of his wife, Ana, and their children rested on what lay beyond that door. As per rehearsed plans, he executed the secret knock—a signal they had worked out for just such an emergency.

Jacob's heart soared with relief as his wife opened the heavy door of the safe room and he was greeted by the familiar faces of his family. His beautiful wife, Ana, and their four young children—his pride and joy—were all there, safe, and unharmed, and he quickly locked the heavy safe door behind him. Ana gasped and put her hand over her mouth to see Jacob's side covered with blood from the flesh wound near his armpit. "It's fine, we'll see to it later," he whispered, as he touched his fingers to his lips to warn them to be quiet, but the sight of them warmed his soul, and he briefly marveled at the unique qualities that each of them possessed.

———————

His two daughters. Emma, 8, and Sarah, 4, bore a striking resemblance to their mother, evoking fond memories of his in-laws in Europe, whom he held in high regard. The girls had inherited not only their mother's looks but also her grace and kindness, making them a source of both pride and inspiration.

His eldest son and namesake, Jacob or little Jake, 10, exuded boundless energy and reminded Jacob of his own childhood. The boy's vigor and curiosity were a testament to the resilience of youth, and he had always cherished the moments spent watching his son grow and learn. The youngest son Michael, 4, the twin to Sarah, was the older boy's shadow and sidekick, and kept everyone on their toes with his antics.

Jacob counted himself fortunate that his children were not only healthy but also remarkably intelligent. It was a blessing he never took for granted. In the stillness of their safe haven, he often found himself giving thanks to God for these gifts and praying for mercy, fervently hoping that his family would be spared the many afflictions he had witnessed others endure, particularly the horrors of war that he had seen in faraway lands.

Even though he acknowledged the inherent struggles of the human condition, Jacob had made it his mission to prepare his children for the challenges that lay ahead. Like nurturing an orchard, he had striven to provide them with the strength and resilience needed to weather life's droughts and storms. He had instilled in them the values of hard work, resourcefulness, and a deep sense of family, believing that these qualities would serve as their anchor in times of turmoil.

All of these feelings passed over Jacob in a flash, followed by the realization that he had only a moment to prepare for a serious confrontation with Jesse Cutshall. His heart raced as he turned to Ana, whispering urgently in the dimly lit safe room that Jesse was outside, and they had to act swiftly. He instructed her to grab the AR-15 while he reloaded his trusty nine-millimeter pistol, the same weapon he had unsheathed earlier at the store. They locked the safe room behind them and ascended the wooden stairs, taking care to move as quietly as possible, though the creaking of the steps seemed unnaturally loud in the tense silence.

They were thankful that their underground home had the cupola, a unique feature with a stairwell that led from the underground living area up to the cupola. It was a strategic decision they had made years ago, providing a vantage point for security and a view behind the house. As they reached the cupola, they strained their ears for any signs of Jesse's presence and cautiously looked down the sights of their weapons, scanning the surroundings outside. The adrenaline from earlier still coursed through Jacob's veins, keeping him alert and focused.

To their surprise, Jesse was nowhere near the shop. Max, the dog, was barking even more ferociously. Right away, they spotted the bag of tools Jesse had attempted to steal, now outside the henhouse, a mere 15 feet from the cupola door. Jesse was in the henhouse, a foolish move indeed, especially since, as Jacob had seen earlier, the criminal was unarmed. In hushed tones, Jacob whispered to Ana, conveying his plan to dispatch Jesse without firing a shot, although they needed to be prepared for a potential fight.

Luck was on their side, as Jacob discovered a large pipe wrench protruding from the bag of tools. He picked it up, positioning himself next to the henhouse door, ready to strike. Within moments, the henhouse door swung open, and Jesse emerged, a hat full of eggs in hand, wearing an ignorant grin under dull eyes, pleased with himself, but then a sudden look of surprise, terror! Jacob's heart raced, and the rush of adrenaline surged through him once more as he swung the pipe wrench across Jesse's temple and jawline with all his strength. Jacob was a big man with large arms and the blow caused Jesse's head and body to slam against the doorframe of the henhouse before crumpling to the ground, broken eggs scattered around him. One of his eyes bulged out now, and his jaw appeared dislocated, contorted to the side. He grew still. Jacob quickly bent down to check Jesse's vital signs, assessing the situation before deciding on his next course of action.

The young Cutshall's heart was still beating, but he teetered on the precipice of death following the blow to his head. Jacob's past experiences in combat had exposed him to the harsh realities of conflict, yet he had never been confronted with the task of executing a wounded enemy. Throughout his military service, his many hard lessons taught him that risks were unacceptable, particularly when the lives of others hung in the balance. Now, the demands of this critical moment left him with no choice but to end the life of the now unconscious petty thief at his feet.

This ethical dilemma was unexpectedly complicated by Jacob's conversion to Christianity after his military service, igniting within him a sudden profound apprehension of divine retribution. He turned to his wife, who had been covering him with the AR-15, "Turn away, Ana." Not only did he not want her to witness the gruesome act, but he also had an embarrassing, scared look on his face that he did not want her to see. Looking skyward, he whispered, *"Lord, do with me as you will. I have no choice."* Facing eternal damnation was the price he was willing to pay for safeguarding his family from evil. The look of fear faded followed by a new savage look of disdain. Max continued to bark, more excitedly, even whining a little now.

With Jesse unconscious, his lower jaw grotesquely displaced, he was clearly incapable of defending himself. The act of taking another's life could no longer be justified within the bounds of self-defense, intensifying the moral complexity of Jacob's predicament. *"So be it,"* said Jacob resolutely as he flipped open his trusty pocketknife, a mere 3 inches in length, but razor sharp, its keen blade poised to fulfill the grim task at hand.

It was an instrument that had served him in more humane endeavors, such as dispatching wounded deer or the routine process of slaughtering goats for customers. However, as he severed Jesse's jugular vein with surgical precision, the stark contrast in the supple texture of human flesh from that of its animal counterpart left a disquieting impression. In Jesse's final moments, though unconscious, the young thief shivered and let out a final, soft gasp as his life's essence cascaded forth in a torrent of crimson, pooling up on the ground like a dark window into the great abyss. And Jacob, for just a brief moment, thought he could see the reflection of his own soul and perhaps his salvation sinking in the thick, murky puddle. But, oddly, he felt no remorse, as the threat posed by Jesse towards Jacob's family would never return. Max, without being told, stopped barking. He too, was satiated and could sense that the threat had passed.

Amid the aftermath of this irrevocable choice, Jacob, once again, briefly wrestled with a disconcerting sense of exhilaration, akin to the heightened emotions experienced during a triumphant hunt. His limbs seemed to throb with a subtle electrical charge, and the world around him shimmered with intensified vibrancy—leaves on the trees and the expanse of the sky radiating brighter colors, a newfound vitality. Yet, this heightened state was distinguishable from the realm of hunting, for before him lay the lifeless visage of a fallen man who was the worst kind of neighbor, but a neighbor all the same. In that poignant moment, a sobering realization dawned upon him—an individual, irrespective of their transgressions, retained traces of the innocent child they once were, a poignant reminder that innocence, once lost, continued to reside eternally within one's person. Still, the crucible of combat as a young man had forged in Jacob an unyielding pragmatism, that required decisive action and the brushing aside of emotions in order to get the job done—a necessity when confronting dire and unforgiving circumstances.

Chapter 5: A Prepared Grave

Standing over Jesse, Jacob felt all of these emotions rush through him in what felt like hours but was, in reality, only a few seconds. "Ana, head inside," Jacob whispered firmly with a stern gaze, motioning his wife back to the safety of their home. She couldn't look at the lifeless body but instead looked only at Jacob, in a way that she had never looked at him before. She was afraid, not intentionally, but the fear could not be hidden. It was as if she had seen a hollow-eyed wolf standing over its prey. "Get it together," he said, "It's not safe yet so you need to get back inside and lock up again. I'm going to clear everything and then bury this corpse." He took the AR-15 from her, trading it for the 9 millimeter, and she retreated back into the cupola, locking the trap door hatch above her before descending the stairs. The steel hatch of the cupola was extremely secure, and Jacob was confident that his family would be secure inside the interior safe room.

He raised his AR-15 to the ready position and began a methodical sweep of their remaining structures, as he had done countless times in the military. It was almost early evening nautical twilight, a time when there is just the slightest trace of daylight in the sky, and there was still a thin line of orange on the western horizon. Jacob had rehearsed clearing the barnyard many times while seeking out and 'smoking' racoons that liked to come pillage the animal feed. The barns, repositories of tools, equipment, and memories, were potential hiding spots for unforeseen threats. Maybe Jesse had a friend that was lurking around, and thus far Jacob had maintained silence, as well as the element of surprise. Every corner and shadow held the potential for danger. Finally clearing the entire area, Jacob concluded that Jesse had come alone.

"Very strange," he whispered, "Lester Cutshall, why have you left your baby brother all alone? Couldn't resist the riots and the mayhem, could you? So many poor choices, so many poor choices…"

Outside, the waning daylight cast long, eerie shadows, intensifying the solitude that enveloped Jacob. He muttered to himself, thoughts swirling as he contemplated the daunting task of discreetly disposing of their neighbor's lifeless body. Time, an unforgiving taskmaster, imposed its unrelenting march. After a period of brief introspection, Jacob decided to maintain his vigil for an additional ten minutes, attuned to any signs of encroaching threats. In Army Ranger School, this technique was called, SLLS, "Stop, Look, Listen, and Smell for the enemy."

The minutes crept by, punctuated only by the rustling of leaves in the wind and the chirping of hidden cicadas, creating an unsettling backdrop to the grim duty he faced. Convinced that immediate danger had receded, Jacob steeled himself for the formidable task of moving the lifeless body to its final resting place—a trench he had excavated years earlier using a rented backhoe. In the movies you might see someone frantically digging a hole to hide a body in this situation, but not Jacob. He had holes dug all over his property just in case. The nearest trench was over 300 feet down the back side of the ridge. It was Jesse Cutshall's very own prepared grave.

The descent, shrouded in darkness and strewn with obstacles, unfolded as a formidable challenge, reminiscent of navigating through uncharted territory riddled with relentless rocks, brambles, sticks, and closely spaced trees. With each step, he struggled on, as if in an endurance challenge, shrugging off scrapes and abrasions as mere tokens of the gravity of his mission. The dead body, a somber reminder of the moral quagmire he had confronted, lifeless, inched its way down the unforgiving slope beside Jacob. He felt as if the two were making the journey together, and he was strangely irritated that he was the only one struggling.

Their arduous descent through the rugged wilderness bore silent testimony to the gravity of the choices they each had been compelled to make. Jesse had repeatedly chosen to steal, intimidate, and take drugs, and his choices landed him here. Jacob's life had been one of a sheep dog, protecting the flock during the Global War on Terrorism, protecting his family, and his community. Now he would deliver the wolf to the underworld. After finally dropping Jesse in the hole, he used an old shovel that had been purposely left nearby to make quick work of the task. There was no remorse, just another job done.

Jacob made his way back up the rugged hillside, the difficulty of the terrain offering no more than a mild inconvenience for a man who had seen far harsher conditions in his past. He was back home within a few minutes. He noticed no further signs of lurking criminals, but there remained one last task to complete before dark. Returning to his wife in the safe room, he retrieved their DJI drone equipped with a thermal camera, essential for nighttime surveillance. "The wound on your side?," Ana insisted as soon as she saw him. She had disinfectant and dressings prepared, but it was not bleeding at all anymore.

"Later," protested Jacob. But she was already pulling of his bloody shirt and using a sterile sponge to clean the gash. "You are going to need sutures," now commanding him with authority. She pulled out the staple suture and had him patched up in a matter of 10 minutes. Jacob gritted his teeth and put on a brave face, even grinning to show off during the procedure. The children watched, fascinated, as their dad smiled gently at them. Ana and Jacob did not hide unpleasant things from their children. Instead, they tried to show them how to react calmly and with composure in the face of adversity. Getting hurt, hunting and butchering animals, and even disagreeing with each other was not to be treated as abhorrent, but instead just a part of life.

After disinfectant, sutures, and a clean bandage, Jacob was ready to get back to work. He was in a hurry to get the drone airborne, and he asked Ana to come with him and pull security with the AR-15. As darkness shrouded the landscape, Ana watched as he skillfully navigated the drone above the dense forest.

The thermal images displayed on his controller screen revealed the heat signatures of objects and individuals. She had heard it before, but Jacob took a moment to explain how thermal infrared signatures worked to Ana, describing the varying colors and temperatures that represented warmer and cooler objects and living beings. "On the screen," said Jacob, "heat becomes the primary indicator, a perspective that feels almost surreal in its detachment from the ordinary, almost as if the bright images represent the human soul."

Ana chuckled as she reminded him that he loved to hear himself give classes to others, and often sounded like a narrator from a survival reality show, often repeating himself. He smiled, glad that she was acting normal, especially after having just watched him dispatch Jesse like a wounded animal. She was a pragmatic woman, not given to being overly emotional like most of the American women that Jacob knew.

Jacob directed the drone's thermal camera along the road and surveyed the scene of his earlier confrontation at the makeshift checkpoint on the small county road. The RV was surprisingly abandoned, with no criminals around, no heat signatures at all. *Where are you bastards? Come out, come out, wherever you are.* He circled back towards his house, beginning to lose hope of finding out the location of the threats. However, as he was about to conclude his search, he decided to check on the elderly neighbor's house, roughly half a mile away. *Bingo.*

There it was, the shed beside the neighbor's house burned brightly, casting a stark and vivid heat signature up into the night sky. The thermal imaging also revealed four distinct heat signatures that undoubtedly belonged to armed individuals. Three of them appeared to be looting items from the house, while one person seemed to be working on the neighbors' old ford ranger with a camper top, which was parked in the yard. Jacob's heart sank as he observed two slightly faded heat signatures on the side of the yard, leading toward the dense forest. A faded heat signature meant only one thing, a recently living but now dead and cooling body. "Fred and Eve!," gasped Ana over his shoulder, putting her hand over her mouth to hide her terrified expression. The couple was in their eighties, and Fred had been on an oxygen bottle. They were basically defenseless. Jacob felt the loss of the nice old couple, but he didn't say a word, there was no time for remorse. The batteries were running low so he had to quickly pilot the drone back to their location and recover it safely.

Afterwards, the couple descended the stairs back into the home from the cupola and Jacob entered the safe room to update his gear. Night vision goggles, weapons, his GMRS walkie talkie radio, and extra ammunition were already meticulously prepared in a separate gun safe, and he just had to put the equipment on. "Ana, I'll lock you all in one more time, as I go pull security. I won't leave the area without telling you first." Climbing the stairs to the cupola once more, and scanning the 360-degree view, Jacob pulled SLLS again, listening, looking, smelling for the enemy, this time with his night vision lowered from his helmet onto his eyes. After SLLS, he called his good neighbor Bill, two more miles down the old county road, which was little more than a gravel trail.

Bill was a generation older than Jacob but spry and of the same mindset, and he had a wife, Shannon, as well as two grown children with their own homes and families were all living in a sort of spread out hamlet a couple of miles further down the county road. After making contact, Jacob began, "Bill, this is the first chance I've had to call, but we have at least 4 marauders, criminals, over at Fred and Eve's, and Fred and Eve have been murdered." Bill was cool-headed and the men calmly talked over the situation. While Jacob wanted to hit the criminals at night, Bill had no night vision and convinced him instead to wait until the morning when Bill and his adult son Scott could come along and assist Jacob in taking out the marauding criminals. It was a brief conversation as both men still had many tasks to complete if they hoped to get any rest at all.

After signing off, Jacob decided to close the cupola hatch and head back into the safe room. One of the advantages to building this type of impregnable home was that you could lock down everything and hunker down inside. If the dog detected another intruder, you could simply go out the hidden tunnel and sneak up behind the intruder to take them out.

When Jacob re-entered the safe room, he was feeling somber after sharing the news about Fred and Eve with Bill, but Ana informed him of a positive turn of events. The internet signal had been miraculously restored, a rare event over the past few years, and various news websites were broadcasting the announcement that the military would soon take control of the country and impose martial law. A skeptical hope flickered in Jacob's eyes; he hated the idea of martial law but perhaps the military would intervene and address the most immediate threat posed by the rapidly expanding groups of gangs and marauders.

While Ana put the children to bed, Jacob set up their old laptop computer, thankful that it still had a functioning DVD player to keep the kids entertained with some old cartoons. He wasn't a big fan of TV for kids, but desperate times called for desperate measures. They made sure the children felt secure in the safe room, where Jacob had stored various weapons and ammunition, in two separate gun safes. The fortified room gave them an island of tranquility as the outside world collapsed. They had gravity-fed water piped into a small sink from the buried tanks at the top of their hill, and the only inconvenience was that while the toilet was installed in the safe room, they had not yet finished building a wall and door in front of it. They would have to make do with a hanging sheet as a temporary curtain for now. There was also no bath or shower in the safe room, so in a long emergency, where they could not leave the safe room, they would have to get by with wash cloths only.

Many "prepper" friends had advised Jacob to keep a 24- hour guard watch in this type of scenario, but Max, the dog, would give him plenty of warning of any possible intruder. His prepper friends, however, had not had the foresight of a tunnel from the safe room to a concealed location, and if anyone ever tried to lock them down, Jacob could sneak out and attack from the rear. It was a great system that meant long term security could be achieved without always keeping a 24-hour watch. As long as the dog was on duty and the family was locked in the safe room, they could have peace of mind, knowing their family was protected from any potential threats.

Even so, on this night there had been a homestead intruder at their home and others were in the area, so Jacob was determined to provide extra security himself by keeping watch alongside his guard dog, Max. Once Jacob had again gathered his security gear, he kissed Ana and headed back up to the cupola to keep a lookout. Thankfully the night was very calm and quiet, with a pleasant breeze from the south that smelled like a dry fall, with maybe a hint of a distant campfire. This time he also brought his laptop computer, to check up on the outside situation, since the internet had been restored.

Despite being furloughed for over four months, due to the government shutdown, Jacob was eager to reconnect with his boss on the military base. If the marauders could be dealt with and if he was given the chance, he could offer his expertise and assistance to help restore order in a nation teetering on the brink of chaos. It was a glimmer of hope in the darkness, a possibility that the tide might turn in their favor.

Chapter 6: The Unfolding Mystery

After leaving the military a decade prior, Jacob transitioned into civilian life by finding a job as an AGIS (Advanced Geographic Information Systems) operator. In this role, he utilized cutting-edge technology to gather, analyze, and interpret geographical data, assisting in decision-making processes across various industries. Normally, AGIS operators like Jacob worked in S.C.I.F.s, or Secure Compartmented Information Facilities. These facilities were designed to safeguard classified materials and sensitive data, ensuring that only authorized personnel could access them. It was tedious work that comprised mostly of data entries and double-checking automated entries made by AI. AI usually created more work than it saved because everything had to be double-checked anyways. Even though the job was usually boring, Jacob always knew where U.S. military units were located around the world; every infantry company, every fighting vehicle, every aircraft. These units all had GPS beacons attached and showed up on the GIS network.

Back in the mid 2020's, when the country was undergoing a series of pandemics and odd national emergencies, most federal workers like Jacob were working from home. With his job this was complicated because the location of many, but not all of the military units was classified, and could only be updated from the S.C.I.F. To solve this problem and allow the AGIS operators to work from home like nearly all other federal workers, specially trained IT specialists worked with top AGIS programmers to set up a dual system, where unclassified system operators could double check and update units from outside of the S.C.I.F., but classified units were hidden behind a firewall. Classified units were tracked and sorted by AI, but active duty personnel working in the S.C.I.F. would update classified data. The unclassified and classified data would merge behind the firewall, to give military commanders a complete picture of all military units' locations worldwide. This way, active duty AGIS operators could update the classified unit information while civilian operators could handle the other side while working from their homes. It would have sounded strange years ago, but at some point in the 2020's federal and state office workers began to consider it a human right to work from home and not from the office. It made the civilian operators nearly obsolete, and he was just waiting to be let go, but he never was let go. He did the best he could to do his job from home, but there really wasn't ever more than a half day's work to do.

Jacob had a close friend named Martin Vetro, a "next-level" computer hacker with a penchant for mischief. Martin had been caught hacking the CIA servers as a teenager, just for fun, but instead of putting him in jail, they put him through college and employed him for several years. When Martin had served his commitment, he moved to a house in the country with his wife and three children, and made a lucrative salary by improving internet security for large corporations. Despite their contrasting careers, and the fact that Martin had grown up in the city, he and Jacob shared a deep bond and often teased each other about the stereotypes associated with country people and city dwellers. "Hey Martin, I brought you some eggs, my roosters are in full production," Jacob would say.

"Awesome, the goat milk that you brought was delicious!," responded Martin.

Jacob replied, oh that wasn't from our goats, I milked the bull just for you!"

"Oh you would milk the bull you smart a$$!," said Martin, finally catching on, and laughter would ensue.

However, Martin's hacking skills extended beyond jokes and pranks. One day, after Jacob had been converted to an "at home employee," Martin found out that Jacob no longer had access to secure GIS information. "It's behind a firewall so there is nothing that can be done about it," Jacob said.

"Oh, I bet," said Martin, those military firewalls are impenetrable," and he whistled under his breath, pretending to be impressed. When the military first came up with the idea, it's entire I.T. community was in an uproar, but then much of the workforce realized that they would have a good-paying, easy job working from home. The government workers unions strongly backed the idea and it was a done deal. The nation's secrets would no longer be completely separate, but instead they would be behind a firewall.

A few days later, Martin called Jacob, and told him to check his postal mailbox. Inside it was an envelope with a new password for his existing account, and an additional password for turning on a new map overlay, which shows military units on a map. Jacob was worried and didn't want to go to jail. To his shock, when he entered the new password on his home computer, it showed all of the classified military units along with the unclassified. Jacob was angry, Martin had never been so brazen with him! He sped up the road towards Martin's house in a rage, and nearly kicked open the door before Martin opened it. *"Do you want us both to go to Federal Prison!?,"* he yelled!

"Settle down, settle down," Martin pleaded, not realizing how angry Jacob would be.

"Let's go," said Jacob, shoving Martin towards the office. *"You are going to fix this right now."*

Martin squirmed, *"Dude, dude, I-I-I can't do that."*

"Oh you can and you will!," fumed Jacob.

Martin softly responded, looking at the wall to his left, avoiding eye contact, *"I can't because, you see, well, I used a data entry to go through the firewall, just like you make your GIS updates, the updates can only go one way so you can't get classified data to come out. But the data entry was actually a two-way portal in disguise, almost like an invisible wormhole in space, you can't see it. Instead of being an actual data entry, it's a door, like a hidden door. But you see, the door is behind the firewall, and everything behind the wall stays there, that's what keeps it classified. So, if I remove the door, it would be like stealing something from behind the firewall, and then you get caught."*

Jacob had become quite religious in recent years, so he had become quite good at holding his tongue. Nonetheless, he unleashed a tirade unlike any other, *"you ignorant son of a #$%@@& @#$&&, you are such an arrogant %$^, you think I want to spend my time with your dumb *&^ in *#%$$^& prison ?!"* It went on and on like this for about 15 minutes, and then Jacob realized he needed to step back from the situation, so he walked around for a few minutes in the yard, while Martin sat silently on his couch. It was a very nice modern home for being in the country, and it had a beautiful, relaxing yard. Jacob felt much calmer after a little while, and decided to go back inside. Martin's brain never stopped *thinking, so he sat back at his computer, an idea clicked in his brain.*

Just then, Jacob, burst back in the house, "Stop right there you **&^** genius. You already said that removing the door is an additional risk, like stealing. Don't do a damn thing. I won't touch that overlay, and you just stay away from my job and my internet. You know, I have a lot of sneaking and peaking skills, not to mention shooting, that I learned in the military, and I would never use that on you, but if you want to play #$$& around, then I'll play. This is over right?"

"Yeah, I'm sorry, you're right," said Martin.

"Alright buddy, I gotta get back to work, jeez this is nuts, we're still friends, but I'm gonna need some time," replied Jacob, and he got back in his pickup truck and drove back home, lost in his thoughts. Maybe he had been too hard on Martin, maybe he had been too easy on him. He just wanted to forget about the whole thing, but he had the feeling that this would always be there nagging at him. He hated the idea of being on the wrong side of the law.

Fast forward back to the present day; it was midnight and Jacob had bigger problems. A roving gang was on the loose nearby and had apparently killed his elderly neighbors, Jacob had killed another young hoodlum neighbor, as well as at least three men in his nearby town, which was being destroyed by mobs. Jacob was presently pulling security from his cupola with a thermal scope, mounted on his AR-10, to keep watch. An AR-10 looks like an AR-15, but shoots a larger, longer range .308 round. Jacob was comfortable engaging targets out to 600 meters with his AR-10, which was the perfect range to shoot anything on all of the ridges that he could see from his home. While regular starlight scope night vision would not have allowed him to see or engage targets out to 600 meters, his thermal scope with 5 power magnification made it easy to spot targets at this range, because bodies are generally warmer than their surroundings, especially at night and in cooler weather.

Ana would relieve him in four hours at about 2AM so he had lots of time on his hands. It was a very quiet night and he decided to check his phone. He was amazed to see that his cell phone service was functioning. It was an unexpected boon, given the chaotic circumstances. For several years, as one national emergency after another hit the country, from power grid failures, to pandemics, to industrial fires, and even catastrophic hacking events, cell phones and internet were no longer taken for granted. The internet had been taken over by hackers, scammers, and criminals; part of a dark underworld of black markets, human trafficking, as well as government crackdowns and censorship. Jacob decided to dial the number of his boss, Colonel Mitchell, who worked on the nearby Bullard Air Force Base.

Bullard Air Force Base had gained notoriety for its role as a remote drone operations center, allowing the United States military to operate unmanned aerial vehicles in far-off locations across the globe. Technological advancements had granted the military the capability to pilot these drones remotely, thereby reducing the need for deploying troops into potentially hazardous regions. Recently the military had begun using its B-21 stealth bombers on unmanned flights, a huge step in the history of military aviation. Major Mark Rinehart was one of the B-21 pilots at Bullard Air Force Base. He was also Jacob's brother-in-law, the husband of Ana's little sister, Mia.

As the call to his boss connected, Colonel Mitchell's stern voice came through, barely concealing his desperation and impatience. "Jacob, you need to get your butt into work immediately! The situation is dire, and we require all hands on deck. There's no time to waste!"

Jacob couldn't believe how unreasonable his boss was being. He struggled to get a word in, his voice steady but filled with concern. "Colonel, I understand the urgency, and I am eager to help, but first off, you all haven't paid me for five months because of the shutdown. Plus, there is another complication. Our neighbors have just been murdered by marauders. My family is here, and I can't just leave them behind, gangs and mobs are literally roving around murdering people in my neighborhood!"

Colonel Mitchell's response was cold and unwavering, his tone tinged with frustration. "That's your problem, not mine. I'm living on base, and you should have made better arrangements. We are going to get you paid and you know what's at stake here, Jacob. We are all trying to work FOR THE GREATER GOOD."

There was that term again, 'for the greater good,' why were people using this term more and more, mainly when they were asking too much from someone else, like some kind of excuse for stepping all over people?

Jacob's patience wore thin as he tried to reason with his boss. "Sir, with all due respect, the situation outside is untenable. It's not safe to leave my family here. If we can somehow make the trip within a few days, can my family also live on the base with me?"

Colonel Mitchell's reply was blunt and unsympathetic. "Absolutely not! This is a military base, not a family retreat. In case you haven't heard, we have a global refugee crisis on our hands, and half of our personnel are busy running international refugee camps here on base. There is no room for anyone's family. Listen, you have a job to do, and I suggest you find a way to do it now. Our active duty personnel don't have time to update the GIS anymore; it's getting backed up and out of control. The internet outages mean that it's no longer feasible to work from home. Your career and the future of our nation is on the line here, Jacob. "

Frustration mounted as Jacob attempted to get a word in, but his boss continued to cut him off, making it clear that the urgency of the situation took precedence over personal considerations.

Jacob realized that further explaining the predicament to his boss would be futile, so he reluctantly conceded. "Alright, Colonel, I'll try to come in later this week, if the roads get cleared, but no guarantees. Please understand that this isn't easy for me, there is no law enforcement in my area."

Colonel Mitchell's voice softened slightly as he responded, "I know it's tough, Jacob, but we're all in a tight spot. Stay safe and get here, just get here. You need to do this not for yourself and your family, but for the greater good!"

Okay, my loyalty meter is now on zero. With a curt nod, he replied, "Roger that SIR!," Jacob hung up the phone and turned to Ana, who had come outside and been listening to the conversation. They both let out a sigh of relief as they knew he wouldn't be leaving their family behind.

Ana was the first to break the silence. "Well, that was intense. What are we going to do, Jacob?"

"One day at a time, Ana," he replied. "Tomorrow, I'll be getting together with Bill and Scott to run these Marauders out of here."

Ana took a deep breath, worried about tomorrow, but also realizing that her sister Mia was another concern. "We should check on my sister. She's on the Air Force base, with no way to come home; I hope she's safe there. I've been thinking about her and I'd feel better if she were here with us. Maybe we should go pick her up when the roads get cleared."

Jacob considered Ana's suggestion but had reservations. "I understand your concern, but traveling for the foreseeable future is way too risky. This is not like one of the previous temporary emergencies that we have lived through. There's still that armed gang just down the road. Even if my truck wasn't ruined, it's too dangerous to venture out. There has been a lot of infrastructure damage this time; mobs are tearing the country apart and food is scarce, it's not easy to fix. We need to hunker down at least until there's a stronger military presence to restore order."

Ana sighed, knowing the truth of Jacob's words but still concerned about her sister. "I know you're right, Jacob. But I miss my sister, she is the only person from my childhood that I have left." Jacob gently squeezed Ana's hand.

"I understand your feelings, Ana, but the base is probably one of the safest places right now. It's on high alert, and she's with her husband, who's a military officer. Mark is a confident and skilled Air Force pilot and also one of the toughest and smartest guys I know. Let's wait a bit longer and see how the situation develops. We can't risk traveling until it's absolutely necessary."

Ana reluctantly nodded, trusting Jacob's judgment. "Alright, but we need to keep in touch with her and make sure she's okay. We'll wait for the right moment to bring her home." Ana had an almost irrational fondness for her sister. At this point, Ana had accepted that she would never see her family in Croatia ever again.

Jacob hugged Ana tightly, grateful for her understanding. "We will, my love. Our children's safety is our top priority. We'll make the best decisions for them above everything else."

Jacob and Ana then called and managed to reach her sister Mia on the phone, who reassured them that she and her husband were safe on the Air Force base, which was well-protected. It was a relief to hear her voice and know that she was out of harm's way.

Jacob told Ana that he was also going to take advantage of the internet restoration to study the global situation and figure out what was going on in the bigger picture, and the situation with the U.S. military. "Don't relieve me on guard duty tonight, I am not planning on sleeping," he told her.

"But you need your rest!," she interrupted.

"I was an airborne Ranger," he told her, "We don't need sleep. If I get tired, I will just take a knee and drink water."

"Alright I owe you one," she said, with a coy smile. She was just as beautiful as the day they met, but he loved her more and more each day as they built a life together. Their children were the personification of their love, and their devotion to family was at a spiritual level.

As Ana descended the stairs back to the safe room, Jacob turned his attention to his laptop. On ordinary guard duty, he would have scanned the surroundings all night with his optics, but with Max the dog on duty with him, he felt free to use his laptop. Jacob had not used Martin's illegal link to the classified GIS maps ever since the day that he learned of it, but this evening and in this situation, he needed all of the information possible to make an informed decision about what to do next. He tried mysterious backdoor link from Martin, which had been dormant for years and was shocked to find that "boom," suddenly all of the U.S. troop locations around the world were suddenly popping up on the map and were now at his fingertips.

He poured over the map on his screen, and studied the locations of military hardware and troop deployments late into the night, trying to piece together a clearer picture of the situation. After hours of study, Jacob began to notice patterns and movements that hinted at a coordinated military response to the growing crisis. The maps were like a puzzle, and he was determined to understand how the pieces fit together. There was a lot of movement but what was going on? What was the DOD (Department of Defense) up to? He knew that staying informed and prepared was their best chance of weathering the storm that had descended upon their world.

As dawn approached, Jacob finally closed the laptop, his eyes heavy with exhaustion. The military movements that he had discovered on the GIS map were bone chilling! Jacob felt an eerie shiver creep from the back of his neck down to the base of his spine, as if he could feel the imminent deaths of millions about to occur, and he pictured a thousand faceless reapers descending from the dark mountain tops and the forgotten shadows, sharpened sickles in hand, to unleash a new era of suffering upon the world.

He was lost in thought. Troop transports heading back to every base and every port at this very moment, martial law. What choice is there? It's the only option, America is going up in flames. So, we withdraw our troops from Eastern Europe and the Western Pacific overnight to restore order? Why? YOU KNOW WHY! THIS was the end game; this is what our enemies wanted all along. Every crisis was fabricated, we were all fooled, the entire west was FOOLED. China, Russia, North Korea, Iran, they have been poised for this for years and now they will strike. It was never just about internal politics, social justice, or viruses; it was not even about the economy. It was about crushing the existing structures of the world that had been in place since 1945 and removing the U.S. from the top. A world competition for limited resources and the control of wealth. Had the U.S. been an always benevolent, perfect administrator of world peace, after World War II? Of course not, but who would replace the red, white, and blue, and how many millions or billions would have to suffer and perish in the process? How benevolent would the new administrators of world order be?

Jacob whispered a silent a prayer for guidance and strength, knowing that the days ahead would be challenging, and his family would rely on him to keep them safe, and closed his prayer with an "Our father," but then repeating the words, "thy will be done, thy will be done, Amen," bowing his head deeply towards his knees as a single tear struck the Earth beneath him. It had been a long day.

Jacob had not been a conspiracy theorist, and he didn't believe that there was some cabal, some sinister inner circle that controlled all world events. Instead, it now appeared to him that global rivals of the United States had used their intelligence services, virus manipulation, economic warfare, and disinformation campaigns to undermine the interests of the United States and create or exacerbate existing problems in order to undermine the U.S. and its western allies. He feared that the new powers that may soon be in charge of global affairs would prove to be ruthless and cruel.

After watching the sunrise and scanning the surroundings in the fresh daylight, he left Max on duty and joined Ana in their tiny saferoom bed, where they held each other close for a few minutes, finding comfort in each other's arms and in their shared resolve to face an uncertain future together.

Chapter 7: Neighborhood Watch

As the morning sun filtered into the room, Jacob realized that he had dozed off for about 20 minutes. It was fine because Max, the guard dog, was on duty, and Jacob would have heard if there was any commotion outside. Jacob's thoughts were still clouded with concerns about the state of the outside world, but he knew that he would have to put that aside to deal with more immediate concerns. He groggily checked his off-grid battery voltage, relieved to find that everything was working well.

He was happy that he had gone against the advice of solar installers and kept a 12-volt battery bank that powered the family's lights, a freezer, a fridge, and even some underground passive cooling tubes with 12-volt fans attached for hot weather. For this, he had installed 900 feet of 4 inch pipes underground in a closed loop when they built their home. This along with the ambient temperature of the Earth was enough to make the home cool, and even though it was a hot July, the safe room was very comfortable for the family.

Before starting his day, a sigh of relief and thankfulness escaped Jacob's lips, but he knew he couldn't afford complacency. Turning to Ana, who lay beside him, he whispered, "I'm going to check the cupola, dear. Keep the kids safe." She nodded, her eyes reflecting the same unease that gnawed at him. Ana volunteered to make breakfast in the kitchen, adjacent to the safe room and accessible through the safe room door.

With practiced caution, Jacob retrieved his .308 sniper rifle from the safe and slung it across his back. He also strapped his AR-15 to his shoulder at the ready, gripping it firmly, and ascended the stairs leading to the cupola, his senses keenly attuned to any potential threat. Each step was deliberate, and he meticulously scanned his surroundings, a 360-degree sweep to ensure no danger lurked nearby. He was relieved to see Max wagging his tail, dutifully trooping the line up and down the fence row. He had also brought up a couple of thawed bones for the dog, and some scraps of old bread.

Having secured the cupola, Jacob requested the drone and daylight camera from Ana by calling down the stairs. The need to keep an eye on their surroundings had become paramount, and these tools provided invaluable surveillance. He also asked her to retrieve the GMRS radios, a means of communication with Bill and Scott, patriarchs of the trusted Harris family down the road.

———————

There was a close-knit group of four households in the Harris family, as well as two other homes of good, fairly self-reliant neighbors in the area. There was the Rothrock clan, a boisterous family of five, who lived further past the Harris's and also Henry Black, a single hermit about Jacob's age. Henry Black lived on the next county road, further south, and his house was only reachable by trail from Bill's house. They had all shared numerous social events in the past, and all were able to communicate with GMRS radios. Bill served as the hub of communications for the neighborhood and kept everyone informed. The radios had been a lifeline during uncertain times. Since the Rothrocks and Henry Black lived further away, Jacob could only communicate with them indirectly through Bill.

GMRS radios, which stood for General Mobile Radio Service, were reliable devices for short to medium-distance communication. They provided a secure channel to maintain contact with neighbors and had been a part of their emergency preparedness plan for years. Depending on the wattage, some of these radios could be used to communicate up to 30 miles away, and they could be easily powered or recharged by solar power.

Over the years, the bond between Jacob's family and the nearby "Harris clan" had deepened. They had often gathered for barbecues, shared laughter, and supported one another during challenging times. The mutual trust that had grown between their families was now more critical than ever as they faced the uncertainties of the world outside of their peaceful countryside home.

Jacob's phone would remain on silent for the day, and he had no intention of answering if his boss called. Thoughts of his employer stirred a mix of resentment and frustration within him. He pondered how someone who had once served his country could be so disconnected from the current realities of life in the countryside. His boss's demands seemed out of touch, oblivious to the dangers lurking beyond the sheltered world of the military base. Who was this "Common Good" that the military was now working for; it seemed they were no longer working for the people or the citizens of this country. It was a sad day.

Despite his military background, Jacob had little faith in the ability of either the military or civilian law enforcement to provide help to rural communities like theirs. The scenes from the news that he had gathered online the previous night had convinced him that cities would be the focal point of relief efforts, as they grappled with unprecedented unrest and chaos. The countryside, it seemed, would have to fend for itself for now.

Military forces still had the capability to assist in restoring order and essential services following the ongoing riots. They could deploy troops to provide security, aid in rescue and recovery operations, and help distribute vital supplies. In the aftermath of the turmoil, their organized efforts could bring a semblance of stability to affected areas. However, Jacob knew that these resources were limited, and their priorities would likely align with the preservation of major cities and serve major corporations. It was understood that Amazon distribution centers, manufacturing warehouses, and all manner of shipping hubs already had a military presence. Small private businesses would bear the brunt of the looting and mayhem, and the federal government and big corporations would be the only powers left standing.

———

Jacob was eager to get the drone airborne and find out what was going on just beyond his own homestead. As he released the drone into the air, its propellers whirred, the mechanical hum cutting through the silence of the morning. The sleek device hovered steadily, its camera capturing a bird's-eye view of the surrounding landscape.

Jacob was no novice when it came to piloting the drone. Years of practice had honed his skills, making him adept at maneuvering the device through the skies with precision. Today, his experience would be put to the test as he guided the drone toward the location where he had last observed the marauders, the controller in his hands and a sense of purpose in his heart. He swerved first to the East and then indirectly to the target, so that they would not know his true direction of approach, or where the drone came from.

As the drone soared above, Jacob's relief grew as he confirmed that the marauders were not lurking around but were still at the house where he had last observed them with the drone the previous night. The group seemed occupied with various activities. A couple of them were tending to a makeshift fire, possibly cooking a meal, or simply finding warmth in the chilly morning air. In the clear light of the day, he could see that they were all totally bald, meaning that they were users of the drug ultraquin. The drug gave its users heightened senses, making them euphoric and irritable all at the same time. It would also leave them exhausted several hours after a dose, meaning that they likely had crashed in exhaustion the previous night. The drone was not close enough to identify any of them, and it wasn't clear if they could spot the drone either. They probably had enough supplies already that it would be more comfortable for them to stay at the neighbors' home until they ran out of food or water. Jacob knew that there had been a large water tank there that probably held 1000 gallons, and perhaps enough food for 4 to 5 days.

Jacob maintained a cautious altitude with the drone, keeping it high enough to avoid drawing any attention from the marauders below. The last thing he wanted was to alert them to his surveillance. He continued to monitor their movements, silently noting the number and positions of the individuals. They still seemed unaware of the unseen observer in the sky, a fact that worked to Jacob's advantage.

With his reconnaissance of the marauders' location complete for the time being, Jacob gently adjusted the drone's course and set his sights on the Harris compound, a loose collection of homesteads housing Bill, his son Scott, their spouses and two other families in the Harris line, 8 adults and 5 children in all. They were the closest neighbors to Blue Spring and were located a couple of miles further down the road. Jacob knew the Harris family to be good, reliable neighbors, and he hoped to glean some information on the current situation of their residence and report back to Bill.

As the drone approached the Harris house, Jacob meticulously surveyed the property from above. Everything seemed eerily quiet, with no signs of movement or disturbances. A quick sweep with the daylight camera revealed that the Harris house remained intact, a small comfort in uncertain times. He did note that one of the old logging trails coming in from the rear of the Harris property seemed unblocked by trees, and he planned to let Bill know. It was probably the trail to Henry Black's place.

Jacob skillfully maneuvered the drone to return to its launch point near his home. His fingers deftly manipulated the controls, guiding the device through the skies with the precision of a seasoned pilot. This drone was normally flown with the help of GPS guidance, mainly to compensate for the effects of wind. This time, for some unknown reason, but not surprisingly, the GPS was not working, and he had to fly using "atti" mode, meaning that he had to fight the wind manually as he flew. Luckily, he had practiced for this eventuality many times. With each calculated movement, he brought the drone closer to its destination, thinking to himself what an awesome purchase this had been. It was a real force multiplier, an item that did the work of an entire reconnaissance team, but in a fraction of the time.

Satisfied with his aerial inspection of the area, Jacob reached for the GMRS radio, preparing to contact the Harris family. The connection was established swiftly, and he spoke into the device, his voice laced with a sense of urgency and concern. The radio crackled to life as he addressed his neighbor.

Bill Harris and Jacob, old friends and neighbors, greeted each other with hearty chuckles as they exchanged familiar nicknames.

"Morning, Buck!" Bill called out with a grin, using Jacob's old army nickname. "You sound serious today, something going on out in the world."

Jacob chuckled in response. "Morning, Wild Bill! I was just planning on going fishing in your pond or maybe poaching some of your deer!"

Their joviality faded as they continued, their voices reflecting the gravity of the situation. "How's Ana and the kids, Jacob?" Bill inquired with genuine concern.

"They're good, Bill," Jacob replied, his voice tinged with worry. "But we're all on edge. Just glad we got our safe room, you know? I did a sweep with the drone of your area already this morning. Noticed that the old logging trail behind your son-in-law's house is not blocked, you might want to get on that before some tweakers figure that out."

"Darn it, I told him… Well, he's good to my daughter but no good with a chainsaw, I'll have to get on that."

Bill then shared an update on his own family, speaking affectionately about his wife and kids. The camaraderie between the two men was sincere, having been forged over many years of shared experiences.

As their conversation shifted toward more serious matters, Jacob inquired, "Bill, have you heard from your buddy, the sheriff? We need to know what's happening out there."

Bill's tone darkened as he considered the question. "Sheriff ain't been much help, I'm afraid," he admitted, his voice tinged with frustration. "Last I heard, he was barely gettin' out of a Walmart alive."

Jacob responded, "Walmart, yeah, I was there, looked like it had caught on fire."

Bill's reply painted an even worse picture. "Mobs, Buck. Angry folks, squatters, tweakers from outta town, desperate for supplies. They descended on the store like a plague of locusts, then burned the entire thing to the ground. Sheriff barely escaped with his life. He's hunkered down at his ranch with some of the deputies, trying to refit and keepin' their families safe from marauders. Hate to say it Buck but at least for the time being, the town of Marshall is lost."

Their conversation took a somber turn as they discussed the dire circumstances that had befallen their community. The realization of the extent of the crisis weighed heavily on both men as they contemplated the challenges that lay ahead. Bill's voice crackled through the walkie-talkie as he listened intently to Jacob's update on the marauders and the grim situation that had unfolded just over the ridge. The gravity of the situation hung in the air as their words traversed the electronic waves.

"Jacob, you've got more military experience than any of us," Bill's voice conveyed the weight of the matter. "We're lookin' to you for a plan, my friend."

Jacob responded, firm and confident. "I'll do what I can, Bill. After I do my chores I'm gonna go over my intel and come up with a detailed operation to deal with these marauders. I'll call you back in a couple of hours with more details but here's your heads up: plan on meeting me at the creek junction at 1400 hours, 2 o'clock for you civilian types. Bring your radios, AR-15's and at least 6 magazines of ammo each. 9 mags would be better if you got it. Ana will provide a drone update before we hit the target. We can't afford to wait another day."

Bill concurred over the walkie-talkie, realizing the urgency of the matter. "Sounds good, Buck. I'll have Scott prepare our rifles, and we'll be ready to move."

With a shared understanding of the task ahead, their voices faded from the walkie-talkies, each knowing that the safety of their families and neighbors depended on their collective effort and strategic planning.

In the military, the plan that Jacob had just given would be considered a 'warning order,' basically the situation, mission, and some general instructions like your timeline, equipment, and communications, plus any special instructions such as the need to prepare a drone.

As Jacob descended from the cupola into the house, he cleared the round out of the chamber of the AR-15 for safety purposes and slung the AR-15 across his back, meeting Ana in their home's main living area. He handed her own AR-15 to her, along with several extra magazines, making sure she had the sling snug with the chamber empty and ready until needed. Jacob always showed her how to "aircraft load" a weapon, as he had done in the Ranger Regiment. You make sure the chamber is empty, let the bolt go forward, and then only AFTER that, you insert a full magazine. If you do this properly, then you have a safe weapon, but you can load and fire in a split second. She had trained with him before, and done a lot of marksmanship practice as a child, but never taken a human life.

"Remember, Ana," he said with a firm but comforting tone, "if anything happens while I'm outside, keep your eyes sharp and your aim steady. Aim small, miss small. I'm nothing without you and the kids, stay frosty and shoot to kill."

Ana nodded in agreement, her determination matching his own. She understood the importance of protecting their family and homestead in these uncertain times. Her family in Croatia had lived through similar times.

———————

With the rifle still slung across his back, Jacob headed out to begin his farm chores. The routine was well-ingrained in him – checking on their goats, feeding and watering the chickens, tending to the pigs. But today, he carried the weight of a difficult decision on his shoulders.

As he approached each animal, he dreaded the task of having to choose which ones to butcher or barter. He liked having a big farm with lots of potential, and constantly improving his herds. He found that each year, the genetics got better by selecting and retaining the best breeding stock. At least he could still keep the very best, low maintenance, "easy keeper" animals. Times were changing, and animal feed would become scarce. He couldn't afford to keep as many.

The goats, with their curious eyes and wagging tails, looked up at him expectantly, demandingly even. Jacob knew that some of them would have to go very soon, providing food for his family and also to neighbors in exchange for resources they might need.

The chickens clucked and scattered about as he tossed them feed and kitchen scraps. Their eggs had been a valuable source of sustenance, but now he would need to consider their fate too. There was probably only enough potential feed on the farm for 10 layers, and they had 25. His plan was to let the chickens free range in warm weather but kill wild game in winter and feed that to the chickens. Giving them bug infested carrion and other scraps would also get them a long way. Every ounce of food counted in these trying times.

The two pigs, with their grunting and snuffling, rooted in the dirt for anything edible. They would soon have to be butchered and preserved in the smoker as well as made into hams using a salt cure. They did not have enough food scraps to keep the pigs all year round. It would be delicious survival food but there was much work to do. He planned to butcher them when the weather turned a little cooler so as not to end up with spoiled meat, but with limited feed supplies, he might have to accelerate the timeline.

Finally, Jacob greeted their loyal Anatolian Shepherd, Max, a steadfast guardian of both livestock and homestead. Max's warm brown eyes met Jacob's, filled with an understanding that transcended words. He patted Max's head affectionately. He was his security partner and he relied heavily on him. Many livestock guardian and shepherd dogs tended to go through fences and run off on their own, causing trouble in the neighborhood. Not Max, he was incredibly well-trained. It was as if Max could intuitively sense what pleased and displeased his owners, and he wanted to be loved.

"Good boy, Max," he whispered. "Times are changing, old friend. We'll need to make some tough choices to get through this, but we'll do it together. You are going to love eating wild game and I am going to be spending a lot of time hunting." Max was what you call essential personnel. He protected all of the livestock, and was an amazing guard dog and security "alarm."

Max responded with a gentle nuzzle, as if promising to stand by Jacob's side no matter what challenges lay ahead. Jacob knew he could count on his faithful companion as they faced an uncertain future together.

After chores, Jacob wolfed down a quick breakfast of eggs, some of which Jesse Cutshall had dropped the previous day, which made Jacob shudder for about a quarter of a second. There was no time for that, he kissed his wife and children and gathered his kit in order to deal with the marauders. He knew that Bill and Scott would bring AR type assault rifles, so he grabbed his .308 sniper rifle with a bipod and adjustable 14 power scope, his 9 millimeter pistol, and also prepared the drone for Ana to use as a recon tool, to scout out the marauders' positions. They would all use the GMRS walkie talkies as comms. Jacob gave them an initial call, just to initiate movement.

As Jacob and Bill moved towards their rendezvous point at the old dry creek junction, they communicated over the walkie-talkies and exchanged their concerns about the marauders who had set up camp nearby. Their radios had earpieces so they were saving time by going over the plan as they moved. With their respective families at risk, they knew they had to act decisively. Jacob began outlining a tactical plan.

"Alright, Bill," Jacob said, "here's the plan. We'll meet up where Thin Branch Creek meets up with Riley Creek, then move together up and along the ridgeline, staying concealed in the thick cedar forest. Once we get to a good vantage point, we will set up the ORP (military term for objective rally point), about 300 yards from the objective, Ana will then send up the drone to confirm the positions of the attackers. That drone will serve as our reconnaissance. We need to be cautious and coordinated, moving slowly and silently."

Bill responded, "Understood, Jacob. I've got Scott with me, and we are zeroed-in and ready for anything. We'll be right behind you." Jacob already knew that Scott was a good marksman, but more importantly, he was five years younger than Jacob, in good shape, and a former police officer. Importantly, his skills with an AR-15 were very formidable. It was not the first time that he had faced criminals. Bill, in his early sixties, was not experienced in combat or law enforcement, but he was youthful, competitive, and would not be outdone by the younger men.

As they spotted each other at the creek junction, the trio exchanged a simple nod and continued their trek through the dense forest. They moved in a triangle, with each man about 5 meters from the next, so it would be hard for an attacker to shoot more than one of them if they were discovered or compromised. Jacob couldn't help but feel a mix of anxiety and determination. His family's safety and that of his neighbors depended on their success. He thought about his children, hoping he would see them again after this dangerous mission.

Bill's adult son, Scott, who had grown up in these woods, was alert and ready for action. The importance of their mission weighed heavily on all of them as they carefully navigated the rough terrain. The forest was eerily quiet, with only the rustling of leaves underfoot breaking the silence. Jacob felt the weight of his .308 rifle, held at the ready, his fingers steady just below the trigger, weapon loaded but on safe. Bill shouldered his own AR-15 with a 30 round mag and 2 extra magazines, and Scott followed closely behind, each of the men spread about 15 feet from the next, moving like ghosts. Their eyes searched for potential threats ahead, their senses heightened by the uncertainty of the situation.

The forest canopy cast dappled shadows on the ground as they moved forward, and they were careful not to step on twigs or branches that might give away their position. They communicated with hand signals, relying on their silent coordination to maintain stealth. The cedar trees, with their aromatic scent blowing in the breeze, provided cover and protection, but brambles and logs made the forest floor uneven and challenging to negotiate.

The forest concealed their movements as they pressed on, determined to reach their vantage point. With every step, they couldn't shake the feeling that they were stepping into an unknown danger, but their resolve remained unshaken.

In the dense forest, the air hung heavy with tension as Jacob, Bill, and Scott inched forward, their senses on high alert. The woods were alive with the sounds of chirping birds, rustling leaves, and the chattering of squirrels. It reminded Jacob of something that he had learned overseas many years before. When entering combat, you will often find that the sky might still be blue and beautiful, the air might be crisp and pleasant, and nature will seem to be at peace, and then all hell breaks loose!

As they pressed onward, the bond between the three men grew stronger, their shared determination binding them together. It was like the bond that men share in war, the knowledge that they will put their body and mortality on the line for each other. The weight of their weapons and gear became a reassuring presence, a symbol of their readiness to protect their families and community.

Jacob's heart pounded in his chest, and his mind raced with thoughts of Ana and their children. He knew the risks they were taking, but he couldn't let fear paralyze him. Instead, he put thoughts of family out of his head and channeled his concern into vigilance, scanning their surroundings for any signs of danger.

With a subtle hand signal, a raised palm up in the air, Jacob signaled for the others to halt. They were about 300 yards from the objective (OBJ), just out of sight, sound, and smell. They formed a tight formation, facing out in all directions, hidden from view within the forest's embrace. Jacob removed his hat, and cupped his ear. It was a signal for the other men to conduct SLLS (stop, look, listen, smell). Ana had instructed them to use the GMRS radio to contact her, and Jacob reached for his device, anxiety gnawing at him. "Put your radios on silence," he instructed the others.

"Ana, this is Jacob," he whispered into the radio, his voice barely audible. "We're in position. Send up the drone and report back."

"Roger, sending it up now," she replied. She had learned the term "Roger" from her husband, civilians normally said "copy."

In the distance, the soft whirr of the drone's propellers could barely be heard as it ascended, its camera scanning the area. The drone's footage provided a unique perspective, capturing the beauty of the forest from above while Jacob and the others remained concealed below.

Ana's voice crackled over the radio, "Drone's up, Jacob. I see the neighbor's house, but there's no sign of the marauders. It's clear, but..."

Jacob's heart sank as he anticipated Ana's next words. "But what, Ana?"

"I see the neighbors," Ana replied somberly. "Fred and Eve. They're... they're still there, dead at the edge of the yard."

Jacob clenched his jaw, the murder of Fred and Eve was a testament to the seriousness of the situation, the intent of the criminals, and he knew they couldn't afford to waste any more time.

"We're not dealing with the bodies Ana, there is nothing we can do for them. They stay where they lay. Follow the neighbor's driveway back to the dirt road," Jacob instructed, his voice determined. "Then head west to see if you can spot the marauders. Then, return east and back home before the drone's battery runs out." The drone batteries only lasted for 15-20 minutes per charge, so it was important to be efficient.

Ana acknowledged and began maneuvering the drone accordingly, her eyes fixed on the monitor as she scoured the terrain for any sign of the marauders. The minutes ticked by as they waited for her update, the forest around them eerily silent.

Finally, Ana's voice came through the radio once more, her tone urgent, "Jacob, I've spotted them. Six of them, heading toward the other neighbor's house, Jeb and Laura, the home closest to the state highway, and past the wrecked RV. They're about 1 mile from your location."

"Good job Ana, get the drone home before the battery dies, over and out." Apparently the marauders had failed to get Fred and Eve's old truck started; it was probably out of gas because of the fuel shortages that had been ongoing in recent months.

Jacob exchanged glances with Bill and Scott, a little frustrated but still determined to push through and finish the job. The urgency of the situation was clear to Jacob; they needed to protect their vulnerable neighbors, Jeb and Laura, who had four children, all under the age of nine, and confront the marauders before it was too late. Jacob had tried to get Jeb to take one of the walkie talkies before the collapse, but he had refused. "I'll be fine, Jacob, I'm not going to live my life in fear. Besides, none of us will die until the Lord calls us home."

"The Lord wants you to be ready to stand up to evil," Jacob had told him. "It's in the bible, he wants you to rely on yourself and protect the innocent." It was no use back then, Jeb would not listen, and now he couldn't be warned of the danger.

They started off towards the east towards Jeb's place but Bill and Scott quickly began to have a change of heart as they left Fred and Eve's property, their voices hushed but filled with conviction. "Jacob," Bill spoke firmly, "we're getting farther from our own homes. We're outnumbered, and this is too risky. We've got our own families to protect for the long haul. We can't afford to lose anyone for those neighbors that have refused to work with us in the past."

The men stopped and Scott chimed in, his tone equally resolute. "We've got to think about our own, Jacob. We can't save everyone, especially not now. After all, the marauders are moving away from our homes and back towards the highway, they might even head back to Marshall. If that's the case, it's better for everyone." Jacob paused, taking a long moment to think, closing his eyes. He then opened his eyes wide, looking straight at Scott with a menacing stare and then replied, mockingly, "If 'ifs and buts' were 'candy and nuts' then we'd all have a Merry Christmas!"

It was an old trick that Jacob used in combat situations in the Army. Just as everyone started to let fear and doubt creep in, he would hit them with a funny one-liner, packed with over-confidence. It was a challenge to manhood, primally understood chest-beating and it always got their attention, and made them forget their fear.

"Look guys," Jacob continued, these thugs are going to prey on Jeb and Laura, then they are going to come back for my family, then for yours, and then four yours, sticking a hard finger in each of the men's chests. Ana spotted six, that means two more than were here yesterday. One is probably Lester Cutshall, and he just collects dirtbags like a sticky trap. He and his friends will hit one house after another on this road until we are all dead, or… We can just take them out right now while they are distracted with Jeb. They think that they are the attackers but just as they get their fangs out, we're going to hit them from behind."

Jacob didn't wait for a response, but instead took off at a fast walk through the open forest along the creek bank towards Jeb's place. Bill and Scott looked at each other, sweat beading up on their brows, then they shrugged and fell in line behind Jacob. Jacob made a quick call on the talkies as they moved to let Ana know their plan, and he told her to put a new battery in the drone, and be on standby.

A few minutes later, gunfire erupted through the forest, apparently coming from Jeb's place still one half mile to the East. It started as 3 bursts of fire, answered by several single shots in succession. Apparently Jeb had been prepared and was firing back. Laura wasn't a fan of guns however, and Jeb would likely have to fight one against six, pretty bad odds. The trio began a quick jog through the open forest, as the gunfire continued off and on for several minutes. Jacob led the way across the road, just prior to and out of sight of the house. Jacob barked hasty orders, "Scott, Bill, y'all cover right down the road, I'll cover left as we keep moving, then we will scramble up the hill and end up overlooking Jeb's from behind, let's move!"

The road was clear but the climb up the hill took a toll, and all three men had to sling their weapons across their backs to be able to grab vines, saplings, and brambles and make it up the steep ridge. Being a veteran of the Army Rangers, Jacob knew that taking the high ground was key, and catching the enemy by surprise by hitting them from the least expected direction would hopefully keep them from taking casualties.

Jacob had a sinking feeling as the pace of gunfire began to slow just prior to cresting the ridgetop. As they came over the top, the firing had just stopped and they saw three figures approaching the old one story, white, wooden farmhouse where Jed could now be seen laying in a pool of his own blood, face down and motionless, to the side of the front porch. Jacob silently took up a position behind a thick old cedar tree and motioned to Bill and Scott behind him to take their place behind two other nearby trees. The enemy was within easy range, Jacob's team was elevated above their targets, and they had the element of surprise. Jacob scanned the area and could see two of the marauders already dead along the driveway leading towards Jeb's house. *Three moving towards the house, two dead, where was the sixth!? Had he moved around behind?*

The answer came as a woman was shoved out the front door followed by a man holding her by the hair, with a long filet knife against her throat. It was Laura! She let out a shriek that would haunt the three men for the rest of their lives as she saw her beloved husband face down in the grass. "No, just kill me now, no Lord no!!!," She screamed, and she freed herself only to kneel in her long jean skirt, sobbing next to her husband.

It was Lester Cutshall following her with the knife in his hand, and a rifle slung across his back, smiling now, as the other three arrived at the site of Jeb's body. Jacob motioned for Bill to shoot the first one on the left, Scott the second, and he would take the third. They would try to take out Cutshall last, since his rifle was slung and he only had a knife, making him less of a threat.

Jacob shot first, followed immediately by the other two, all three hitting their marks. Jacob's shot from the .308 sniper rifle went through the base of the skull dropping the man immediately, but the other two were shot with .223, a much smaller round, and because these AR's had iron sights, they shot the men in the chests, giving them a few moments to stumble and thrash about, trying to get up on to the porch.

Lester Cutshall took advantage of these moments of confusion, and grabbed Laura by the hair, dragging her back inside before the three men could get a clear shot at him. "Damn, gotta go now, let's go," said Jacob, as they bum-rushed down the hill. Luckily, Lester did not turn back for a shot at them and they successfully reached the cover and safety of the outside wall of the house without being fired on.

"Stack on me," Scott forcefully ordered, his law enforcement training taking over as he prepared to lead the men into what had become a room clearing operation, with hostages involved.

There was no hesitation, and the men burst into the empty living room, blood on the carpet, a broken table in the middle of the kitchen. They immediately restacked and flowed into an empty living room, just in time to catch a glimpse of Jeb and Laura's old Subaru peeling out of the driveway on the back side of the house! They were powerless to stop the vehicle as it rounded the corner and disappeared. "Finish clearing," commanded Jacob, but it was no use.

The men quickly realized that the home was empty, toys still strewn about, dirty dishes on the table. Even the children were gone. Jacob, Bill, and Scott looked at each other, faces flushed, mouths dry. The adrenaline rush hadn't yet started to fade, but they all felt sick to their stomachs, with the image of Laura screaming still in their heads. That and the unknown status of the children were all they could think about. "Maybe they had the kids loaded up when the criminals arrived, or else they just came back to get supplies. Jeb always had said that he would head down to his parents' house further south if things got really bad," said Jacob.

Scott checked the back side of the house, "Jeb's truck isn't here, there's nothing we can do without a vehicle, we can't help Laura now" he conceded.

"I'm burning it down," said Jacob, pulling an old zippo out of his pocket and lighting up the curtains.

"Wait what, but hold on…," protested Scott, but it was too late.

"Let's beat feet," said Jacob, "skedaddle, move the f@*$ out and keep your head on a swivel, this place is a combat zone," ordered Jacob. He had switched fully back into Army Non-commissioned officer (NCO) mode, and his two neighbors were falling in like a couple of good soldiers. The place was empty, and Jacob knew that leaving the house intact would only invite more marauders to come back, especially with Lester Cutshall still on the loose.

Burning down possible enemy assets was also something that Jacob had learned overseas; vehicles, homes, shacks, if the enemy could use them, he was going to burn them.

On the way out Jacob told Bill and Scott to watch the road while he stepped into Jeb's tool shed. He quickly, found what he was looking for, "you were a good man, Jeb, thanks for helping me one last time," said Jacob as he hefted a 20-inch, fueled-up Stihl chainsaw up on to his shoulder.

Jacob led the way to the south edge of the yard and cut a more direct route on their withdraw, staying low towards the creek instead of the ridgeline, but staying just off the road. Flames from the burning home began to lick the sky before the three had even reached the creek 200 yards away. Jacob quickly radioed Ana as they approached the creek bank, taking a left and heading back east towards the homestead. They moved along a different route and remained concealed on the way back to avoid any likelihood of further contact.

Three times along the way back, Jacob turned in towards the county road and cut down a few large trees, felling them across the entire roadway, while the other men pulled security. He was extremely cautious with chainsaw safety, and glad that he had spent hundreds of hours using a chainsaw before the collapse. With no outside medical help available, even a small injury could turn into a deadly infection or a permanent crippling disability. The county road was now closed, and hopefully no more marauder traffic would be coming their way. Bill and Scott were sweating profusely now, emotionally, and physically drained.

Despite all of the death and tragedy that occurred, Jacob felt good, colors looked more vibrant somehow and he felt young and more alive, just like when he was serving in the military. The feeling of combat to an experienced soldier is like the best coffee and cigarette buzz you can ever imagine. Your mind is focused, your muscles are pumped, and if you have prepared yourself properly, then you are spiritually confident, knowing that you are doing the best you can to be 'just' in an imperfect, and at times, a wickedly twisted world. It had been years since Jacob had felt this way, but the worry he had felt for days was gone, now replaced by confidence and determination.

The men marched on, back towards their families, and despite the tragic loss of Jeb, and the kidnapping of Laura, they would all be just a little safer now. When they reached the creek junction that had been their original rendezvous point, Jacob turned to the other two men, who were visibly exhausted, but Jacob caught a hint of their unexpected elation and relief that they felt at being alive still after the harrowing ordeal.

"There it is!," said Jacob, "you feel that, that strength, you men did good, those kills were justified! We depend on each other now, we are not neighbors, we are brothers."

Bill nodded enthusiastically and replied, "Thanks Jacob, you know we're always ready to answer the call with you. Scott and the family are all staying with his mom and I now, so you know where to find us. Call me anytime, day or night," said Bill.

The men shook hands with and looked each other in the eye. They were of one mind, one tribe. As the trio of Jacob, Bill, and Scott reluctantly parted ways, they each retraced their steps through the dense forest, heading back to their respective homesteads. The air was thick with the earthy scent of the woods, and the early evening sunlight filtered through the leaves, casting long shadows all along their paths.

———————

Jacob's presence as he walked disrupted the tranquility of the forest, causing a deer to bound away with a start. He watched the graceful animal disappear into the underbrush but made no move to give chase. The prospect of fresh meat wasn't a pressing concern; he hadn't the time to process it and it was too warm to let it hang for long. His main focus was securing his family's physical safety right now.

Using the GMRS radio, Jacob signaled Ana that he was nearly back. The walk back was uneventful, allowing him time to reflect on their situation. He thought about their neighbors, Fred, Eve, and now Jeb, and the somber reality of their loss settled heavily on his shoulders. Nonetheless, he was at peace, knowing that he had done everything that he could to bring security to their home, their sacred Blue Spring Farm.

Upon reaching his earth-sheltered house, Jacob approached the cupola, where Ana had maintained her vigilant watch. Her eyes lit up when she spotted him, and a wave of relief washed over her. They shared a long embrace, taking comfort in each other's presence.

With the immediate threat seemingly at bay, they decided it was secure enough for the children to come out of the safe room, and play in the rest of the house. They eagerly retrieved their toys and began playing as if nothing had ever been wrong in the outside world. The sounds of laughter and whispered conversations filled the air as they resumed a semblance of normalcy.

Chapter 8: A New Normal

The next few days were quiet, with Jacob placing a call to his old boss to let him know that he would not be in to work anytime soon, as the roads were impassable. His boss was furious but Jacob could not have cared less. Cellphone service went down in the middle of the call, and Jacob doubted that it or the internet would be working again, at least anytime soon.

Instead, Jacob busied himself along with his son Jacob junior, or Little Jake, butchering the hogs. It was a huge job and Jake, 10 years old, was a strong boy and great help. Jacob had been worried that it was too warm and that the meat would spoil, but they had no more food or enough scraps to feed the hogs. They worked quickly and had all of the meat either safely in the smoker or in the freezer within 90 minutes of slaughter. Meanwhile, Ana and 8 year old Emma were busy with milking, canning vegetables, and making more butter and cheese. They were fortunate to have both a 12 volt refrigerator, and freezer that provided them with storage for milk and other perishables. Most people in their part of the country relied on grid power, which had now failed, but at Blue Spring Farm, they were off grid. The twin babies Sarah and Michael were just beginning to milk goats, but their main job at only 4 years of age was just to play and not get hurt.

About a week after the incident with the Marauders at Jeb's house, in the middle of the night, the Starlink internet suddenly came back to life.

A mere two years earlier, the U.S. Government had nationalized the Starlink company, and it had since become free but also notoriously unreliable. It was ironic because the government takeover was part of a law passed by congress that declared access to information to be a human right, and internet was to be given to all free of charge. With no profit incentive for internet providers, the existing infrastructure began to fail from lack of maintenance, computer glitches, and malicious viruses.

As Jacob sat up in the dimly lit room, unable to sleep, the soft glow of his laptop screen illuminated his anxious face. His family lay asleep, unaware of the disturbing news that unfolded before him.

The first news story that caught Jacob's attention, confirming his theory, was a shocking 'days-old' announcement from the American president. The United States had completely withdrawn its troops from Eastern Europe, leaving its allies in Poland, the Czech Republic, and Romania on their own and vulnerable. Ukraine had already been occupied by Russia for years now. This new decision sent shockwaves through the international community, leaving many Eastern European nations feeling abandoned and exposed to potential threats. They were reaching out to form alliances with Russia within hours of the announcement, striking pipeline deals and making security concessions, kings were being made while others were toppled with each passing minute.

The second main headline was equally unsettling. The American president had declared the postponement of elections for two years, which would effectively extend his term in office to a full decade. The implications of this move raised concerns about the erosion of democratic processes and the consolidation of power in the executive branch.

The third piece of news was about the significant redeployment of American military forces in the Pacific. Troops and naval forces in and near Japan, South Korea, the Philippines, and even the American territory of Guam, would be pulled back closer to Hawaii and the west coast of the United States. Guam was suddenly declared an independent nation. The president cited the need to bring U.S. forces home to help restore order and rebuild the country.

With the United States leaving the western Pacific, the balance of power was rapidly shifting. Chinese forces were already starting to take the island of Taiwan, and the absence of American deterrence would mean that the takeover would occur without much resistance. Besides Guam, the Northern Mariana Islands, and American Samoa, U.S. territories which had relied on the United States for protection in the Pacific, now faced an ultimatum, cozy up to China, or be run over by them. The Philippines would also be on its own in the South China Sea. Australia's economy was almost as bad as that of the U.S., so they were in no position to fill the power vacuum. Australia had immediately been making overtures for an alliance with China.

Jacob continued to scroll through the headlines, deeply concerned and feeling the weight of the unfolding events. As he delved deeper into the news, he stumbled upon a series of alarming reports about the state of American cities. The devastation caused by the recent riots and criminal takeovers, which had already taken a toll during the pandemics and anti-police protests of the last decades, had now escalated to unimaginable proportions.

City after city had been plunged into chaos, with buildings set ablaze, streets littered with debris and burnt vehicles, and storefronts shattered beyond recognition. Dead bodies had not even been removed from most of these scenes. The estimated cost of the damage was staggering, surpassing the billions incurred during any previous riots. It was irreparable damage, easily representing trillions of dollars gone up in smoke. An apocalyptic wave of destruction had swept across the nation.

The images accompanying these reports were haunting; charred remains of once-thriving businesses, iconic landmarks reduced to ashes, and streets teeming with desperate people and refugees. In some cities, the population was attempting to return to a semblance of normal under the watchful eye of new gang and cartel overlords who were armed with heavy machine guns and armored vehicles. The scenes were reminiscent of war-torn cities in the middle east or the Ukraine of years past, a stark contrast to the vibrant urban centers they had once been.

Jacob couldn't help but feel a sense of despair as he absorbed the magnitude of the crisis unfolding in his own country. The news stories painted a grim picture of a nation in turmoil, struggling to contain the chaos within its borders.

The strategic movements of military forces that Jacob had pieced together were beginning to reveal a larger and more sinister plot. It became evident that the BRICS nations, long jealous of U.S. power, through a calculated global shift from American dollars to Chinese yuan, had already succeeded in virtually eliminating American influence on the global economy. Now the American economy itself was collapsing.

These same influential global forces were also the ones orchestrating the removal of American military presence from bases around the world, ensuring that an economic defeat would be followed by a military one, and all without a single shot being fired. This had been the Chinese plan for years, but few had believed they could execute it so flawlessly. Russia was just a tool and a supplier of resources to China at this point. The question that loomed was whether there were insiders within the American government actively facilitating these developments, and how high up they were in the government. Jacob felt like no one in any part of the government was even conducting counterespionage anymore, let alone hunting spies and traitors. Years ago, such activities were deemed paranoid and outdated.

As Jacob delved deeper into the global situation, he couldn't ignore the looming resource shortages plaguing the world. The concept of limited energy supplies haunted discussions, with available world oil reserves steadily dwindling and prices making the commodity unaffordable in most places of the globe. Fleets of idle vehicles littered streets with no fuel to power them, and the electric car was a luxury item reserved for the ultra-rich within global safe zones, such as the south of France, Dubai, or the area around Washington D.C. Areas like these had well-funded private armies that had protected the rich elites.

Current and predicted oil reserves and refining capabilities painted a grim picture of future scarcity, setting the stage for heightened competition and conflict over the world's dwindling fossil fuel resources. But it wasn't just oil; fertilizer chemicals, including phosphate rock fertilizer, were becoming increasingly scarce, posing significant challenges to global agriculture. Additionally, rare earth minerals and various metals essential for microchips and manufacturing were in short supply. The world was grappling with the stark reality of finite resources and an ever-growing population. The "haves" would be few and powerful, and the poor miserable "have nots" would be the overwhelming majority. It was if the slums of Calcutta, India were combined with the ruins of Aleppo, Syria, and that had now become the model for most cities across the globe.

The past decade had witnessed significant fluctuations in the price of phosphate rock and other fertilizer, reflecting the growing concerns surrounding its availability. Prices had surged as demand outstripped supply, and the scarcity of phosphate rock had become increasingly evident. For decades, the world had consumed and relied on millions of tons of phosphate rock fertilizer every year, a staggering amount necessary to sustain global agricultural production. However, these reserves were now nearly exhausted, leaving humanity on the precipice of a critical shortage. The world had been fed for decades by relying on record crop yields that were attained only through the heavy use of chemical fertilizers such as phosphates. Now, the timeline for when this invaluable resource would completely run out was becoming a looming question mark, heightening fears of food scarcity and geopolitical tensions over control of the remaining finite reserves and control over food itself.

China, with its insatiable hunger for resources, was at the center of these global struggles. The Chinese need for oil, fertilizer chemicals, and rare earth minerals was insatiable, but the world's supply was far from sufficient to meet these demands. As China was quickly displacing American influence around the world, it aimed to redirect these precious resources away from the United States and into its own rapidly expanding economy. Through strategic alliances, economic coercion, and territorial expansion, China had almost completed seizing control of key resource-rich regions including much of Africa and Latin America, thereby ensuring its uninterrupted access to the vital materials needed for its continued growth and dominance on the global stage.

The question that gnawed at the core of these unfolding events was whether China's grand strategy could be successfully executed without triggering open international warfare or even a nuclear conflict. Would the U.S. and indeed the entire west withdraw from power without a shot fired? It appeared that this was already happening.

Chapter 9: Securing the Perimeter

Jacob knew that securing the homestead was essential, and having access to his truck, now out of fuel with a punctured fuel tank, could be a game-changer. Despite his reservations about going back out on the county road and risking an encounter with marauders, he decided it was worth the risk. After a many uneventful days of work securing food supplies, with no more signs of intruders, he finally decided to undertake the task. There were only 250 gallons of diesel fuel in the spare farm tank, so, besides this task, it would only be used to save lives, escape danger, or get medical attention.

For tasks like these, when Jacob was not at the homestead, it was decided that Ana would stop chores and pull security. Young Jake had done plenty of shooting, including a few successful deer hunts, and he was gradually learning his role as a rifleman on the homestead as well, out of necessity.

Jacob pulled the old John Deere tractor out of the shop and made his way down the driveway and up the county road to the old pickup truck, which had served them faithfully for years. He put a chainsaw behind the seat and was well-armed, taking his AR-15 and wearing an old Army LBE (Load-bearing Equipment). It consisted of a thick equipment belt, 2 canteen pouches, a small first aid pouch, a compass pouch, and two magazine pouches carrying 6 x 30 round magazines total. It was a 1990's old style rig, not as fancy as the chest rigs that he had worn during most of the war on terror, but it made him feel oddly nostalgic and it was comfortable enough.

The truck was located on the near side of the trees that Jacob had dropped in the road earlier, so those would not obstruct his path. He arrived within a few minutes and dismounted the tractor. As he approached the vehicle, he couldn't help but reminisce about the countless times that the old gray truck, a Ram 1500 with a long bed and a Cummins diesel engine, had been used for family outings, trips to town, and even the occasional fishing expedition. But now, it held a different kind of value – one of survival.

The first task was to tie the steering wheel in a straight position. He found a sturdy piece of twine in the truck bed and carefully secured it, ensuring the wheels wouldn't veer off course during the tow. Next, he fetched tow straps and began the process of hitching the truck to the tractor. Jacob had insisted years ago on adding a tow hook package to the truck so one strap was easily wrapped around the hooks, one on each side, then routed through the tow bar of the tractor, and then the loops were closed with two shackles.

The job was a little cumbersome while carrying the AR-15 and equipment belt, but he was back up in the tractor and facing the right direction within a few minutes. He had placed the truck in neutral, ensured the brake was released, and began pulling slowly as the old truck smoothly fell in behind him. As Jacob carefully maneuvered the tractor with the truck in tow, he couldn't help but feel a sense of relief that he hadn't encountered any more criminals along the way.

All of the trees that they had dropped along the way had certainly helped keep people out, and though there was a backway to town in the other direction, Bill and Scott had blocked that one as well. Even so, Jacob stopped two more times on the way back to his driveway to drop a few more trees to add on to existing obstacles behind him, ensuring no one could get to their home without a considerable amount of effort. There was a rough old logging trail that Jacob could repair and then use to cut cross-country and get to the highway once his truck had been fully repaired, but he didn't want to go to town under the current conditions anyways.

On his way back up the hill. His heart raced, and he muttered silent prayers of gratitude under his breath, thanking God for his many blessings and the safety of his family in these perilous days. Finally, he reached a flat spot next to the house where he could park the truck. Despite the physical exertion and the August heat, it was more his nervousness from making a bunch of noise down on the road that caused him to sweat profusely. The knowledge that Lester Cutshall was still out there, and certainly allied with yet another group of criminals, weighed heavily on his mind.

Jacob didn't waste any time. He hurried back into the house to check on his family. Everything was secure but after making so much racket towing his truck and using the chainsaw, there was one essential security measure that he decided would be prudent. First, he told Ana to continue to pull security, in the case that he had been followed.

Then, Jacob decided to set up an OP or observation position, about halfway down the 1200 foot long driveway, on a rocky but concealed perch overlooking the gravel public road below. Ana had again gathered the children and put them in the safe room, and he was proud and thankful that she understood the importance of security and took it seriously. Jacob knew that Ana was more than capable of handling the situation, and would probably be fine, even if something happened to him. After all, she had grown up in the war-torn region of Bosnia, the daughter of a Croatian sniper during the conflict that had ravaged the country.

He thought about his wife's unique past while he overwatched their quiet country road, which seemed so far from the chaos of America's cities. The war in Bosnia had been a brutal and devastating chapter in modern history. Ethnic tensions had erupted into violence, pitting Serbs, Croats, and Bosnians against each other. Ana's family had faced unimaginable challenges during those tumultuous times, and she had grown up tough and resilient, shaped by the harsh realities of a combat zone.

Ana's early years were marked by hardship and struggle, as she and her family had to adapt to a life of uncertainty, where danger lurked around every corner, and hunger was often at the doorstep. It was an upbringing that had instilled in her a deep sense of self-reliance and the ability to face adversity head-on.

Despite the challenges, Ana had managed to acquire valuable survival skills and a level of resourcefulness that would prove invaluable in the uncertain days ahead. Jacob trusted her implicitly and knew that she would do whatever it took to protect their family.

As a young non-commissioned officer, Jacob found himself deployed to the war-torn country of Croatia, as a peacekeeper, serving in the aftermath of the devastating conflict between Serbia and the Bosnians. It was a tumultuous period in the Balkans, marked by ethnic tensions and lingering hostilities. His mission was to conduct reconnaissance and gather critical intelligence on the ground, assess the situation, and aid in the peacekeeping efforts.

One day, while stationed in a small Croatian village near Vukovar, Jacob heard rumors of a local legend—an enigmatic figure known as "The Iron Eagle." The townspeople spoke in hushed tones about a fearless marksman who had single-handedly defended their village against Serb forces during the darkest days of the war. Intrigued by the tales, Jacob decided to investigate further.

His inquiries led him to a modest farmhouse on the outskirts of the village. It was there that he met Ana for the first time. She was a striking young woman, her gentle face filled with a combination of resilience and sorrow. With her dark hair and piercing blue eyes, she was very slender, but had an aura of strength that immediately captivated Jacob.

Ana's family had endured immense hardship during the war. Her father, a skilled sniper, had become a local hero for his unwavering commitment to protecting their community. He had instilled in Ana the values of courage and determination, and also taught her to shoot with unparalleled precision.

As Jacob spent more time with Ana and her family, he couldn't help but be impressed by their self-reliance and the warmth of their hospitality. Despite the scars of war that marred the village and the lives of its residents, there was a sense of hope and unity among the people.

Jacob's mission took on a dual purpose: gathering intelligence and offering support to the villagers. He collaborated closely with Ana's family, and together, they worked to rebuild their shattered community. In those challenging days, bonds were forged that would endure long after the war had ended.

Ana and Jacob grew closer as they shared stories of their respective experiences and aspirations. She shared tales of her father's heroism and the sacrifices her family had made to protect their home. In turn, Jacob spoke of his commitment to serving his country and his longing for a world free from conflict, even if he had to create a small world of his own on a small family farm. She loved the idea, and a shared vision was born.

Their connection deepened into a profound friendship, and as the war-torn region slowly began to heal, Jacob and Ana found solace and strength in each other's company. Their love story was one that crossed boundaries of nationality and culture, born from the ashes of war, and nurtured by a shared desire for peace and a brighter future.

In time, their friendship blossomed into a love that transcended borders and boundaries. Despite the challenges of their different backgrounds, they recognized in each other a kindred spirit, bound by their unwavering commitment to building a world for their family that was yet to come.

As the sun began its descent, moving down towards the horizon and casting long shadows through the forest, Jacob knew it was time to do more to secure the perimeter of their homestead. He headed back up the hill to their protective earth-sheltered home, imitating the call of a bobwhite quail to let Ana know that he was on the way. It was one of their pre-arranged, secret signals. With the threat of marauders lurking nearby, he needed to take every precaution to protect his family.

After saying hello to the children, and adjusting his gear, he carefully pulled out a box with a set of ready-made traps that were triggered by trip lines. These ingenious devices had been acquired through an online purchase made before the economic troubles began. They were designed to set off shotgun shells by means of a device that Jacob had modified for their needs. However, handling these traps filled him with a sense of apprehension, as he was all too aware of the potential danger they posed to his own safety.

Moving with deliberate stealth, and taking the traps and the shotgun shells with him, Jacob ventured into the dense woods that bordered their property. His heart pounded in his chest as he navigated the uneven terrain, all the while being sure to avoid accidental misfires of the traps. Each step was measured, each placement of the trip lines methodical, with a careful eye toward ensuring that they wouldn't interfere with the movement of their farm animals, keeping them outside of fenced areas and especially anywhere that the children would possibly play.

His hands were steady as he set the traps in strategic locations, approximately 100 meters away from their homestead. He knew that the consequences of making a mistake could cost him a finger, an eye, or worse, and he couldn't afford any missteps. The eerie silence of the forest, punctuated only by the occasional rustle of leaves or the distant call of a bird, heightened his sense of vulnerability.

To bolster their defenses further, Jacob also replaced the batteries in and readjusted hunting cameras equipped with FM transmitters along the perimeter. These cameras would transmit images back to their homestead if any activity was detected, providing an additional layer of security. The choice of where to install these cameras was guided by his understanding of potential threats and the most likely approaches that criminals might take.

Some of the cameras were strategically positioned near game trails and natural chokepoints, where intruders would be most likely to pass. Months ago, Jacob had dropped trees in the wood line around his home, leaving gaps in the fallen rows of trees where trespassers would find it easier to pass. Others were discreetly tucked away near potential entry points, such as ridgelines, gates, or near old trails leading towards the road. The quiet woods, once a source of tranquility, had become a place of uncertainty and vigilance.

With each trap set and each camera positioned, Jacob felt a growing sense of accomplishment. He was determined to defend their homestead against any threat that might emerge from the shadows. As darkness settled in, he made his way back to Ana and their children, ready to face the challenges of the uncertain days ahead.

Returning to their home at dusk, a wave of relief washed over him as he reached the cupola where Ana was on guard duty. Max barked loudly, not recognizing Jacob at first. She looked up from her post, her face illuminated by the soft glow of the laptop screen in the dimly lit cupola.

"Welcome back," Ana greeted him, her voice hushed. "Phone service is still down, but our Starlink is back up. We just received an email from Martin."

Jacob nodded as he took a seat beside her, his eyes scanning the email on the screen. Martin's messages always carried an air of urgency.

Chapter 10: One More thing to Worry About

Martin's email was written in his typical cryptic and cavalier tone. "Greetings, my friend. I hope this message finds you well. I have made a decision to return to my home in Costa Rica. My recent endeavors have been rather fruitful, allowing me to maintain an expensive second home in the beautiful tropical countryside. There are larger moving pieces in world events that need my attention. The world may be on the brink of nuclear warfare. I trust that you have made use of my tools that I left you. From my location, I don't have the same visibility that you have, so I am asking you a favor. Let me know if your brother-in-law goes on vacation to the Western Ocean anytime soon. This will help me decide if I will continue my own stay here on the Gulf Coast. Oh yeah, and check on my house for me, I know it's several miles from yours but if you know any quality people that want to stay there when I'm gone, that would be great! 'Pura Vida,' signed, your friend, Martin."

The vagueness of Martin's message left them both a little puzzled but Jacob got the idea. Martin wasn't trying to be cagey, but there were things that he couldn't risk saying online. Jacob knew his friend's knack for reading between the lines, and when Martin spoke of "larger moving pieces," it was a signal that something significant was afoot.

"Smart bastard bugging out to Costa Rica!," exclaimed Jacob.

"What could he mean by my Air Force brother in law going to the Western Ocean?" Ana wondered aloud. "And why the sudden urgency?"

Jacob ran a hand through his hair, deep in thought. "Martin has always been one step ahead when it comes to world events and technology. If he's leaving, it's for a good reason. We should take his words seriously."

They began brainstorming potential scenarios and threats that Martin might be alluding to. It could be related to political tensions, global conflicts, or an unforeseen crisis that threatened international stability.

Jacob began to think aloud, "Mark is a pilot of strategic nuclear bombers, and if Martin is concerned about that, it means that there is a possibility that a deployment will happen. If so, then this all means that the movement of U.S. forces out of Eastern Europe and the Western Pacific might not only be for the purpose of implementing martial law in the United States. Perhaps the pentagon is also planning on deploying forces to a new location. But if the U.S. is out of money, how will they even afford the deployment?"

"China!," Ana interjected. "The Western Ocean is China's name for the Indian Ocean! China might actually transfer funds to prop up the current administration and the U.S. government if the pentagon does it's bidding."

"Right, of course!," Jacob responded, "For years U.S. foreign policy has always strangely benefitted China, how should this be any different. But it's on a whole new level, it's the ultimate Sun Tzu Jedi mind trick!"

"Sun Tzu Jedi?," asked Ana; her English was excellent but this had her stumped. Jacob explained, "Sun Tzu is the author of the 'Art of War,' a Chinese manuscript dating back to around 500 B.C. The premise is knowing when to fight and when not too, and it gives countless techniques for manipulating and misleading the enemy. So, if you are China, then the ultimate Sun Tzu trick would be to get the deadliest fighting force that the world had ever seen, in this case the U.S. military, to fight your battles for you. China has long coveted the influence and resources that India has harnessed in what they consider to be their 'Western Sea.'"

Ana interjected again, "Didn't China just lease a large port and open a military base in Sri Lanka?"

"Bingo!," Jacob exclaimed, excitedly almost as if playing a game, "China doesn't just want Sri Lanka, they want it all!"

"Bingo?… Jedi, mind trick?," asked Ana coyly.

"These are not the droids you're looking for," answered Jacob, right on cue, and they both started laughing, releasing the built up tension from so many weeks of bad news. "You are so cute," said Jacob, "I feel like I've been too busy to even stop and look at you in these past weeks," pulling her in a close embrace now.

Ana clung tightly to her husband, unable to ignore his masculine presence, the wild look of his sunburnt face, and the muscular bulk of his hardworking body. He was like a wild predator, finely tuned and always poised and taught, like a mountain lion, and she was happy to be his prey.

"No time for that," said Ana smiling and pushing him away, heading down the stairs into their home. We need to prepare," Ana said, trailing off as she continued down.

"Damn prepping habits," Jacob mumbled.

"What did you say," asked Ana from the bottom of the stairs.

Regaining his composure, Jacob replied, "Uh, um, well yes, you're right, I just said that it might be time to stock up on supplies for a longer haul."

Ana agreed, her mind racing with possibilities. She walked halfway up the stairs, "Let's check our food and water stores, ensure our extra solar panels and battery electrolyte are ready for use, and review our security measures. We should also contact our neighbors, Bill and Scott, and give them a heads up. Oh, and stock up on more fishing items..."

Jacob replied, "Yes, totally, I'm on it, I'm glad that we are so busy that we don't even need to stockpile birth control!" The couple stopped and looked at each other, and then instantly cracked up with laughter!

Chapter 11: More Prepping

As they continued to focus on their preparations and potential courses of action, the uncertainty of the future loomed large. Martin's enigmatic message had set them on a path of readiness and vigilance, determined to protect their family and face whatever challenges lay ahead.

In the following days, Jacob and Ana began strategizing about how to make their resources last. With the specter of nuclear warfare hanging over their heads, they knew they needed to be self-reliant, and stocked up to the brim. One concern was food, and Jacob believed that in a major nuclear conflict, they might face a nuclear winter of 5 years or more. He had tried to have enough food stockpiled for that many years, but maybe it was time to add more to that, maybe try for 6 or 7 years.

"We will have to butcher some more of the goats," Jacob suggested, his voice grave, sitting around the breakfast table one morning. "We can smoke or salt the meat to preserve it, and ration it carefully."

Ana nodded, her expression mirroring the gravity of the situation. "And the vegetables from the garden – we'll need to harvest and can as much as possible before it's too late. We might not ever be able to rely on the outside world for help anymore."

They spent hours each day working diligently, stockpiling supplies, and fortifying their homestead. The routine of farm chores had taken on a new sense of purpose as they braced themselves for the uncertain times ahead. They also took care to prepare their 7500 gallon concrete rainwater cistern for the possibility of nuclear conflict. This meant re-routing the gutters that had been set up to turn the cistern into a rainwater catchment. In a nuclear conflict, rainwater can deliver radioactive nuclear fallout material into any water supply. Even though 7500 gallons meant only 4 gallons per day, Jacob knew this would be enough for just drinking water and his water pumping windmill could supplement them for other needs.

In the stillness of the countryside, just over the ridgeline where the home sat, the distant sounds of gunfire echoed ominously, emanating from the direction of the state highway, which led from the nearby military base to the town of Marshall.

With a sense of urgency, Jacob rushed to prepare their trusty drone for flight. The highway was 4 miles away, at the far end of the range of the drone, and he knew the drone was their best chance to gather information about the source of the commotion and whether it posed any immediate threat to their homestead. As the drone soared into the sky, its camera relayed a live feed to Jacob's smartphone.

The scene that unfolded before him was both chaotic and reassuring. A convoy of military vehicles, including armored personnel carriers and Humvees, was engaged in a fierce firefight with what appeared to be some kind of checkpoint or roadblock that someone had set up, probably some kind of vigilantes, maybe someone like Lester Cutshall. Jacob had not noticed this checkpoint before and it was hard to see what was going on because the drone was at its limit of communication and could not get closer. Seeing the military moving down the highway on a clearance mission indicated a determined effort to restore order and eliminate marauder and gang activity, which was a step in the right direction!

As the drone continued to hover at a safe distance from the scene, capturing the intense firefight, Jacob noticed that the military forces were making quick work of dismantling the makeshift checkpoint. They had an olive drab military bulldozer that immediately moved in pushing away burning tires and a broken down car, among other refuse. It was clear that they were well-prepared and well-armed, showing no mercy to the marauders who had disrupted the area's stability.

Low on battery, Jacob piloted the drone back to his homestead. It had been weeks since Jacob and the family had been holed up at Blue Spring, and maybe now some semblance of law and order would make things safer for everyone. With a sense of relief washing over him, Jacob contacted Bill on the GMRS radio, unable to contain his excitement. "Bill, you won't believe what we just witnessed. The military is here, and they're taking down what appears to be an illegal marauder roadblock and checkpoint near the highway!"

Bill's voice crackled with emotion as he responded, "Jacob, that's incredible news! We've been holding down the fort here, but just remember that we put up our own roadblocks on the gravel country road. I don't fully trust those military folks and they won't like our roadblocks. You should probably steer clear of them for a while. They don't know friend from foe right now.."

Scott chimed in on his own radio, his relief evident. "We've been living in fear since this all began. Seeing that the military is trying to take back control is good, but we don't know what their orders are."

"I concur," said Jacob, "just remember that soldiers are just regular people, and most of them have good intentions. Still, I'm glad we are off the beaten path, let them fight the criminals up in Marshall, and once things settle down, we can think about a neighborhood resupply, maybe."

The news of the military intervention spread quickly among their GMRS network of trusted neighbors, and a cautious sense of optimism permeated the tight-knit community. While the sight of military forces brought reassurance, it was also a stark reminder of the widespread devastation that had befallen the more populated areas.

As the sun dipped below the horizon and the evening settled in, Jacob and Ana watched the drone's footage once more, this time together with their children. They explained the significance of the military's arrival and tried to alleviate the fear that had plagued their young minds. It was another example of how their parenting differed from other parents. There weren't any bodies or any close action in the videos, but they wanted the older children to know what was going on and how the world actually worked.

For the first time in weeks, a glimmer of hope seemed to have pierced through the veil of uncertainty. While the challenges of the post-disaster world still loomed large, the knowledge that the cavalry was coming, ready to restore order and provide assistance, offered a renewed sense of purpose and determination to the resilient homesteaders.

As they sat together in their safe room, a sense of relief washed over them, knowing that the marauders who had once posed a significant threat to their security were likely eliminated or at least were back on their heels. The military's presence in the area, as demonstrated by the dismantling of the illegal checkpoint, signaled a shift in the balance of power.

Over the next several days, there was no more sign of activity from the direction of the highway. Jacob and Ana threw themselves into a steady routine of self-sufficiency, focusing on essential tasks that would sustain their family in the uncertain times ahead. Each day began with them rising before the sun, their children still wrapped in blankets of sleep. The homestead echoed with the clucking of chickens and the bleating of the goats, a symphony of farm life that served as a reminder of their self-reliant existence.

Butchering animals became a high priority, a reminder of their responsibility to provide for their family's sustenance. With rifles close at hand, Jacob and Ana worked in tandem, efficiently processing the meat of their goats, ensuring that not a scrap would go to waste. They carefully separated cuts for immediate consumption and those destined for preservation.

Smoking meat was a time-honored tradition that Jacob had mastered over the years. He prepared the cold smoker with hickory chips, the fragrant smoke enveloping the meat as it slowly took on a rich, smoky flavor. Ana, meanwhile, was in charge of salting and seasoning the meat before it was hung in the smoker. This meticulous process would extend the shelf life of the meat, providing a vital source of sustenance throughout the year.

Their garden had yielded an abundant harvest, a testament to their foresight and diligent care. Root vegetables, including potatoes and onions, were carefully harvested and stored in their root cellar. The cool, dark environment of the cellar would keep the vegetables fresh for months, a crucial addition to their winter provisions.

Amid their agricultural efforts, Jacob and Ana took turns watching over the homestead with rifles ready, a constant reminder of the world's unpredictability. Luckily their dog

Max would alert them to the arrival of any stranger, although their home was so remote and the climb to reach it was so steep, that they had not had any visitors since the incident with Jesse Cutshall. They cherished the brief moments when their children could play outside, under the watchful eyes of their vigilant parents and loyal guard dog Max.

In addition to their regular chores, they spent hours each day rotating their goats to fresh pastures, ensuring that their livestock could graze on nutrient-rich forage. This practice not only kept their goats healthy but also preserved their precious hay reserves for the harsh winter months. Luckily hay had been harvested, baled, and stored away in the barn mere weeks before the total collapse that occurred in July. It was September now and cool evenings were a reminder that green pastures and green leaves would soon give way to fall color and frosty fields.

The days seemed to blur into one another, filled with the comforting rhythms of homesteading. Ana and Jacob also turned to other homestead skills, Ana knitting warm scarves and mittens, while Jacob honed his carpentry skills, repairing and improving their homestead structures, livestock pens, and fences. Their resourcefulness knew no bounds, as they adapted to a life that felt both archaic and essential.

The most anticipated time in September was the apple harvest. The couple had planted apple trees when they first moved to the property, and these were finally producing a bountiful crop. They chose the Arkansas Black variety, because of its resistance to local fungi and blight. From their original 25 trees, they were harvesting around 2000 apples this year, giving them lots of surplus to make into apple cider, apple butter, and apple pie filling. The pie filling would be canned or stored in the freezer, enough for one pie in each jar or bag. All of the children and the dog came to the orchard, just 200 feet downhill from their home, for the apple harvest. They all enjoyed romping around, chasing each other, and filling up laundry baskets full of apples to haul up to their home.

Their world may have changed dramatically, but in the midst of uncertainty, Jacob and Ana found solace in the simplicity of their self-sustaining lifestyle, taking comfort in knowing that they had the skills and determination to provide for their family, no matter what challenges lay ahead.

Communication via cellphone and Starlink was almost always down now, so they had no idea what was going on in Marshall let alone in the populated areas of the nation. In truth, they didn't want to know, but were in a way glad to be isolated from the hard realities that were certainly being faced by the less prepared. With martial law now imposed, Jacob had also been afraid to use his uplink to the military GIS maps. He basically considered himself no longer employed by the military as his boss had stopped contacting him.

As August turned into September, and green leaves began to yellow, the family felt a transformation in themselves, from modern citizens into something more primal, more like pioneers, or homesteaders in a new unknown dark age.

Chapter 12: International Stirrings

A couple of weeks later, as the days grew cooler in late September, Starlink internet had briefly been up a few times, and global news was a mixed bag of hope and concern. Jacob and Ana were able to gain valuable insights into the evolving global and local landscapes. From the news reports, it was clear that the repositioning of American military forces from foreign bases to domestic soil was proving to be a double-edged sword. On one hand, it brought reassurance that disaster relief and infrastructure rebuilding were slowly underway, instilling a sense of security. On the other, the realization that American cities were still grappling with armed gangs of looters and marauders underscored the grim challenges faced by the nation.

Of particular note on the global stage was the ongoing conflict between the Indian and the Chinese Armies along their contested border regions. China had already finished mopping up in Taiwan, annexing the once Democratic nation. This, combined with the withdrawal of U.S. forces from most of the Pacific theater, meant that China could reallocate its forces to its western frontier and along the border with India. The disputed border had long been a flashpoint for tensions, but recent escalations were cause for apprehension.

News reports hinted at skirmishes, territorial disputes, and an increased military presence along the border, stoking fears of a broader conflict. Similarly, along the Pakistani border, there were reports of a village of Indian Sikhs that were massacred by Pakistani militants. Jacob couldn't help but ponder the implications of such hostilities on the global stage, knowing that instability on one side of the world often had far-reaching consequences. He wondered if this had anything to do with the email that he had received from Martin that had referenced the Indian Ocean.

———————

Closer to home, the news regarding the nearby town of Marshall painted a picture of both hope and containment. Bill had recent radio contact with his friend the sheriff, and had learned that the imposition of martial law had, in some ways, restored order to the beleaguered town. The military's efforts to distribute food and clean water, along with the establishment of tent camps for residents, provided a glimmer of optimism. There was a sense that the government was attempting to stabilize the situation, albeit through stringent measures. The sheriff had relinquished most of his power to federal authorities, and was assisting them in any way possible. He had been reluctant, but with the scale of the crisis and the size of the military force, he felt that there was no other choice. He did tell Bill that he would try to give local leaders and residents a heads up if there was any heavy handed moves by the military that would affect them.

The military had also established an outdoor prison camp for individuals caught looting, and military trials were underway in Marshall. The emergence of a makeshift justice system raised questions about civil liberties and the rule of law in these troubled times. Jacob and Ana couldn't help but grapple with the implications of such actions, understanding that maintaining order came at a cost.

———————

On the first day of October, in the middle of the night, Ana's cellphone rang unexpectedly. She didn't know if she was more surprised that cellular service was working or that it was her 23 year old sister Mia, who lived at the not-so-distant Air Force Base, on the other end of the phone. She was sobbing and hard to understand.

"I can't understand, Mia, speak clearly because we could lose signal at any moment," Ana pleaded.

Mia composed herself, "Ana, Mark has been deployed, I don't know where they have sent him and I'm trying to get to your home, I'm at the highway but the road is blocked."

"Oh no Mia," Ana replied desperately, "I told you to stay on the base where it's safe. Are you alone? You know our road is blocked totally by trees."

"I know Ana, but the base is locked down so strictly, it's awful and they've brought in extra ground troops and started quartering them in our homes! They are from out of state, and not trustworthy. A friend of Mark's one of the garrison commander's aids, has taken me this far in his jeep, but now we're blocked, I need your help!"

"Just sit tight Mia, pull off the road and Jacob can be there in maybe 30 minutes," instructed Ana before hanging up the phone.

"I heard everything, I'm on the way!" said Jacob.

———————

This is exactly why Jacob had retrieved the truck and had found time over the past several weeks to patch up the fuel tank and fuel line in his truck. The diesel engine easily started and roared to life for the first time in two months. The trail was narrow, and Jacob already had the chainsaw loaded. He would not be taking the gravel road but instead would take an old logging trail that had also been blocked with a few downed trees, though fewer than the road. After clearing the trees all the way to the highway, and successfully navigating the rough trail in the dark for 4 miles, he finally reached the rendezvous point at 4 AM. There he was to meet with his sister-in-law and the friend of his brother-in-law, whose name was Jeff.

Just as Jacob pulled up his truck, a third vehicle, an old military Humvee also pulled in, hit the brakes, and skidded to a halt, with a spotlight instantly trained on Jacob, Mia, and Jeff. "Hands where we can see them!" a soldier shouted over a loudspeaker.

"I'm active duty," yelled Jeff, "relax!"

Two soldiers dismounted and jogged over with their weapons raised, "let's see some ID," one of them shouted. Jacob and Mia kept their hands in the air while Jeff flashed his ID. "Okay, sorry captain, this is Indian country around here." He then turned to Jacob, "You two live here, I thought most people in this area were dead, do you have food supplies?"

Jacob quickly realized he wasn't offering them food; he was looking for food. The sergeant's cheeks looked gaunt, and his eyes were a bit glazed. "No sergeant," Jacob replied, "we are half starved ourselves, do you have any food to spare?"

The sergeant replied "No sir, but you look just fine, you don't look hungry. People in town have almost nothing left and government stockpiles are empty, we are taking, um, taking donations from farmers in the countryside if you have any."

"No sergeant, not farmers, I'm an IT worker and I'm all out of food, this Captain was kind enough to bring our stranded daughter back home." He used the term daughter because she looked young and he wanted to be protective as he didn't trust the sergeant.

"Okay sir, carry on then, let's move out!," shouted the sergeant, and he hopped back in the Humvee, and just like that, they were gone.

Jacob hugged his sister-in-law, "let's get you home to safety!" "I can't thank you enough Jeff, how can I repay you; do you need anything?," he asked the captain.

Jeff, shook his head, "I have to get back to base, we are all locked down indefinitely, and I don't want to get in trouble with my commander. These days if you get in trouble, you are more likely to get shipped out to the Indian Ocean. Oops, I didn't tell you that," he laughed nervously.

"Is that where everyone is going?," interrupted Jacob. "Nope, got to go, good luck everyone," and Jeff hopped back in his vehicle and raced back down the highway in the direction of the base.

"Let's get out of here before the next patrol comes along," he said to Mia, and they drove back into the forested trail. Jacob stopped 4 times on the way back to use the chainsaw to drop more trees on the trail to keep anyone from following them. Luckily, in this part of Arkansas, there were big hardwood trees everywhere and each one was a potential roadblock.

———————

Mia's unexpected arrival left Jacob and Ana in a state of shock. Ana's little sister, with whom she had many fond memories of childhood, was now grown and newly married, standing before them, her eyes filled with tears and her heart heavy with the weight of her husband's deployment. She had made the risky journey to reach them, her fears of potential military lockdown and draconian rules for military families driving her to seek the safety of her sister's home. It was a bittersweet reunion that tugged at their hearts.

As Mia regained her composure, she revealed the classified information that her husband had shared with her before departing. He had been deployed to Diego Garcia Island, a remote outpost situated in the middle of vast expanse of the Indian Ocean. The very mention of the island conjured images of isolation, mystery, and a top secret military base located on a tropical island. It was a place where nations could assert control, where military might intersected with geopolitical interests.

Isolated and far from prying eyes, Diego Garcia served as a vital hub for the United States military, one of the few that had not been abandoned after the recent collapse of the American economy. The base's strategic location allowed it to function as a critical refueling and resupply point for military aircraft and naval vessels crossing the vast distances of the Indian Ocean. It was a place where warriors and warplanes found a temporary home, a respite in the midst of challenging missions. And now, it was the place where Mia's husband would carry out his duty, far from the familiar comforts of home. The news of her husband's deployment to this remote outpost sent ripples of concern through the family.

———————

As Mia and Ana caught up, speaking their native Croatian, Jacob couldn't help but ponder the underlying reasons behind this unconventional move by the U.S. military. Strategic bombers, especially the new B-21, are typically stationed within the United States, and possess the range to execute long-range missions from American soil. The decision to deploy them thousands of miles away to Diego Garcia Island hinted at a shift in military strategy, a departure from the norm, or even an intentional folly.

One theory that lingered in Jacob's thoughts revolved around the escalating tensions with China. Recent developments, including the Chinese occupation of Taiwan following the withdrawal of US forces from the region, had stirred apprehension on the global stage. The deployment of strategic bombers to such a remote location might be a signal of readiness—a message to potential adversaries that the United States was prepared to respond swiftly and decisively to emerging threats, a kind of rear guard action. The complex dynamics of global geopolitics were at play, and the family found themselves affected by it, searching for answers in an ever-changing world.

Whatever the implications, Jacob was happy to find that the Starlink was up, and as Mia and Ana continued their banter in Croatian, Jacob fired off an e-mail to Martin. He gave his old computer hacker friend the heads up that he had requested, and perhaps paid him back for giving him the illegal window into top-secret troop movements. In the e-mail, Jacob concocted some story about his new friend Diego Garcia that he had met at church. It was a code that he knew Martin would understand. He didn't know if he would ever see his old friend again, but Jacob hoped that he and his young family were safe, and perhaps he might again provide Jacob with some critical and timely information at some point in the future.

Amid the swirl of questions and concerns, the family took solace in Mia's presence. After a few hours of sleep, now in even tighter quarters in the safe room, they woke early for a rare, long, family breakfast. Reuniting with her little nieces and nephews, they shared laughter and fond recollections of the times that they had spent together before the economic crisis and social turmoil had made travel unsafe. Silly games and shared secrets from Ana and Mia's childhoods in Croatia resurfaced, serving as a bridge between their past and their uncertain future. The playful banter and easy camaraderie between family provided a momentary reprieve from the weight of the world outside their home.

For Jacob and Ana, Mia's return was a testament to the enduring strength of family bonds. The world may have been in turmoil, and their circumstances far from ordinary, but the love and connection within their family remained unbreakable. They knew that the road ahead would be challenging, and that the mysteries of the wider world would continue to unfold, but they faced it together, fortified by their unbreakable bond.

After morning chores that day, Jacob, determined to gather more information about the deployment of strategic bombers and troops to Diego Garcia, retreated to his laptop and launched the ArcGIS mapping program. He was hoping that the internet would work just one more time. ArcGIS was a tool he had used extensively during his military career, and even though he was using an illegal back channel created by his friend Martin, he knew it would be invaluable in his quest for answers.

The history of Diego Garcia was an intricate tapestry of geopolitical maneuvering, military strategy, and global interests. The United States had maintained a strategic presence on the island for decades, using it as a forward operating base to project its military power across the Indian Ocean region. While the base had primarily served as a logistical hub and a refueling station, its significance extended far beyond its remote location.

The deployment of bombers such as the B-21 and B-2, to Diego Garcia may have been linked to the escalating tensions in the region. These long-range bombers possessed the capability to carry out a variety of missions, including strategic nuclear deterrence and conventional strikes. The decision to station them at such a remote outpost hinted at a strategic shift, possibly a sign that the U.S. was about to pick a side in an emerging conflict involving the Indian border regions. What side would they pick, and what sinister international forces would determine that choice?

―――――――

Since the internet was working again, Jacob delved deep into the classified side of the ArcGIS mapping program, and he scrutinized the recent movements of US Air Force assets in the region. He discovered that aerial refueling tankers and reconnaissance aircraft had already been making frequent sorties from Diego Garcia, suggesting a high operational tempo. These activities hinted at an increased surveillance of the Indian Ocean and the broader maritime theater. Jacob found that the surveillance missions were not being flown anywhere near China at all, but instead they were being flown in and around Indian airspace.

While this theory provided a plausible explanation for the deployment of Mark, Mia's husband, it left Jacob with lingering concerns about the potential risks involved. The conflict growing around India involved multiple nuclear-armed powers, and the implications of an escalating conflict in the region could be dire. Jacob knew that the situation called for continued monitoring.

His curiosity piqued by these new developments in the Indian Ocean, Jacob expanded his research to global news stories. The world seemed to be on the precipice of significant geopolitical shifts, and he wanted to understand the broader context.

One thing that caught his attention were strange news articles detailing the development of tensions rising between India and the United States while, paradoxically, China and the United States seemed to be agreeing not to engage in any further discussion over Taiwan. It was a diplomatic shift on the part of the U.S. that defied easy explanations. Jacob was even more astonished to find that the U.S. was allowing the tiny island of Guam, until recently a U.S. Territory, to lease its military facilities to China, now that the U.S. had withdrawn and granted the island independence. This would have been unthinkable just a few years prior.

As he delved deeper into the matter, Jacob learned that the U.S. Secretary of State had embarked on a high-stakes mission to Beijing, aiming to smooth over relations between the two superpowers. The timing was impeccable, considering the simmering tensions that had previously been high between the United States and China over Taiwan, the South China Sea, economic disputes, and cybersecurity concerns.

However, what truly boggled his mind was the sudden escalation of tensions between the United States and India. Historically, the two nations had shared common interests in countering the influence of China in the region. They had engaged in defense partnerships, participated in joint military exercises, and fostered diplomatic ties. But something had shifted dramatically over the past few months while the U.S. economy was in turmoil and major U.S. cities had been nearly burned to the ground.

Mainstream news posited that economic disputes and trade imbalances had begun to sour the relationship between the United States and India. Tariff battles and disagreements over intellectual property rights had strained their economic ties, creating an undercurrent of mistrust. The U.S. was blaming India for a fertilizer and petrochemical shortage, claiming that Russia and India were cutting the U.S. out of important trade deals involving primarily the agricultural industry, but also petroleum. This came at the worst possible moment, when many Americans were facing a food shortage, and for some reason India was being painted as the scapegoat in the media. As economic pressures mounted, so did the diplomatic friction, and national resentment. It would have been unthinkable just a few years earlier that India would ever be seen as an enemy of the U.S., but now it was happening! The question was why! The media's explanation just didn't add up.

Was it possible that India's growing assertiveness in the South Asian region had raised eyebrows in Washington, or was it more likely that someone or some nation was exerting an outside influence on the policy makers in Washington. India's border disputes with China, Pakistan, and Bangladesh, as well as its expanding military capabilities, had positioned it as a formidable player in the Indo-Pacific. The United States, wary of a potential power shift in the region, might have sought to exert more influence over its strategic ally. Or perhaps it was a malevolent foreign entity, namely China, that was using the United States to check the power of India. China had already used its 'belt and road' policy to turn Sri Lanka into its newest vassal state, just off the coast of India.

This culmination of these tensions led to what Jacob perceived as a precarious situation. The possibility of a conflict involving the United States, India, Pakistan, Bangladesh, China, and possibly even Russia, FIVE NUCLEAR-ARMED NATIONS, was a grim specter that hovered on the horizon. The implications of such a scenario were profound, with global repercussions that could reshape the geopolitical landscape of the entire planet, even causing a world war, or nuclear apocalypse. In Jacob's eyes, this was a recipe for Armageddon.

Jacob delved further into the specifics of the disagreements between India and the United States, trying to discern the flashpoints that might escalate into a full-blown conflict. One major area of contention lay in the realm of trade and commerce. The United States had accused India of trying to nationalize American businesses and assets located in India, alleging that Indian regulations placed unreasonable restrictions on American businesses operating within the country. Disputes over tariffs, taxation, and intellectual property rights had soured trade relations and caused severe economic strain between the two nations. Some U.S. businesses were threatening to shut down operations within India, and several U.S. businessmen and U.S. tourists had been mysteriously murdered recently in the country as well. Looming large were also India's growing energy demands. It had established partnerships with countries like Iran and Russia to secure sources of oil and natural gas. This had raised concerns in Washington, which sought to curtail India's reliance on nations that were at odds with U.S. foreign policy objectives.

Furthermore, Jacob uncovered simmering disputes related to technology and defense. India had expressed interest in purchasing advanced Russian military equipment, including the Su-57E, fifth generation stealth fighter, a move that irked U.S. officials more than anything. The United States viewed such purchases as compromising interoperability with allied forces and jeopardizing sensitive intelligence sharing.

As Jacob continued to scrutinize the evolving geopolitical landscape, he couldn't help but notice another surprising turn of events in U.S. foreign relations. The longstanding complexities of the South Asian region had led to shifts in alliances and diplomatic maneuvers. Most notably, the relationship between the United States and Pakistan had improved dramatically. Pakistan, historically a contentious partner, was now successfully lobbying the United States to support its territorial claims in the Kashmir region.

The Kashmir issue had been a longstanding source of tension between India and Pakistan, with both nations staking claims to the region and engaging in sporadic conflicts. Historically, the United States had maintained a position of impartiality, advocating for peaceful resolutions through dialogue. However, the recent shift was seismic, as the U.S. government began to openly endorse Pakistan's territorial assertions over Kashmir. This marked a significant departure from its previous stance and hinted at broader geopolitical realignments in the region. It also played into the hands of China, that had its own territorial claims on land currently controlled by India.

For Jacob, this development was nothing short of shocking. The unpredictable chain of events had painted India, the world's largest democracy, in a new and negative light, as it found itself at odds with the United States. The implications of this shift were far-reaching, raising concerns about potential conflicts, alliances, and the precarious balance of power in an increasingly volatile global arena. As he pondered the unfolding situation, Jacob realized that he needed to remain vigilant and adaptive, as the dynamics of the world continued to shift beneath his feet. Martial law, potential nuclear conflict, not to mention a huge mobilization of U.S. citizens for military service were now all real possibilities.

Chapter 13: A Return to Normalcy?

In the next few weeks on Jacob and Ana's homestead, fall turned into early winter, and they began to return to a semblance of routine and normalcy. The daily chores of taking livestock to fresh pastures, harvesting late crops like squash and potatoes, once disrupted by unforeseen events and uncertainties, were gradually settling back into familiar patterns. Each day brought with it a renewed sense of purpose and self-reliance. Fortunately, they had heard through Bill's friend, the Sheriff, that order was mostly restored in Marshall, although people were still without power and low on food.

The animals on the homestead, a key part of their homesteading journey, were once again grazing contentedly on fall-stockpiled pastures. The goats, with their voracious appetites, provided milk and meat, while the chickens continued to lay eggs faithfully. Jacob would feed the chickens mainly with carrion and food scraps now that the vegetation was retreating for the winter. Ana would often venture out with the children to gather the eggs, a task that was both rewarding and educational for the youngsters. They would also gather fat wormy acorns from the nearby forest, and throw those into the chicken coop to add to their diet. At least there had been a bumper crop of acorns this year. Even though the nuts were a potential survival food, Jacob and Ana's pantry was already overflowing with flour, beans, cornmeal, and canned goods. They had plenty to eat, just consuming items that were due to expire soon.

In preparation for the impending colder months, Jacob turned his attention to the extensive woodlot that surrounded their homestead. Armed with a chainsaw, he began the laborious task of cutting firewood. Luckily, he had stockpiled nearly 100 gallons of regular gasoline, which would last a long time if just used for the chainsaw. He had purchased non-ethanol fuel and would use a commercial fuel stabilizer to keep the fuel good potentially for up to two years. The rhythmic hum of the chainsaw echoed through the forest as he carefully selected trees for felling. With practiced precision, he ensured that each piece of wood would fit snugly in their woodshed, providing a reliable source of warmth for the coming winter. Jacob junior, the oldest child at 10 years old, was now responsible enough to pull security for his father while Jacob used the chainsaw. He would even occasionally kill squirrels, possums, or armadillos with his .22 rifle. He had been taught the fundamentals of marksmanship and gun safety, and he took the responsibility seriously.

Their garden, though still yielding a decent fall harvest, required diligent attention. The remaining root crops, carrots, and fall squash, were carefully tended to, with Ana and Mia working side by side, while 8 year old Emma watched the twin 4 year olds. As they harvested their crop, they meticulously sorted and stored it with the produce in their root cellar—a hidden gem beneath the earth, in the back, windowless side of their earth-sheltered home, maintaining a cool, dark environment that would preserve their bounty for the months ahead.

Foraging for wild edibles became a cherished family activity. Jacob, with his extensive knowledge of local flora, taught the children which mushrooms were safe to eat and which should be avoided. They ventured into the nearby forest in search of berries and nuts, often returning with baskets brimming with nature's sweet treats. They had recently enjoyed an unusually late crop of Chanterelle mushrooms, and now that the first frosts had hit, they were in search of sweet, juicy persimmons. Some of the persimmons were eaten immediately but others were pounded into a thin pulp, and then dried and preserved as fruit leather, by placing them in the open wood cookstove oven, at about 125 degrees, for 5-6 hours to dry. In normal times this may not have compared well to snacks from Wal-Mart, but in hard times it seemed like a magical Candyland treat to the children.

As the days flowed into weeks, the routines of the homestead offered a comforting stability in a world fraught with uncertainties. Jacob and Ana found solace in their self-reliance, knowing that their resilience and resourcefulness would continue to sustain them in the face of whatever challenges lay ahead.

Jacob's resourcefulness and determination knew no bounds. He had long harbored a dream of converting an old broken down four-seater ATV into an electric vehicle (EV). Over the years, he had collected the necessary components—a powerful electric motor, custom gears, and a 6 KWh lithium battery. It was a project born out of a desire for a silent and efficient mode of transportation on their homestead, that would rely on power from their solar panels instead of from an outside fuel source.

The heart of the project lay in the integration of the electric motor and gears into the ATV's chassis. Jacob meticulously disassembled the ATV, carefully making modifications to accommodate the new components. He welded custom mounts and brackets, ensuring that the electric motor was securely attached and aligned with the existing drivetrain. It was a meticulous process that required precision and skill, but Jacob was up to the task. The easy part was space. The existing motor, transmission, coolant, and exhaust system were all removed, leaving plenty of room to work, as the electrical components were much smaller. Once the brackets were secure and aligned, attaching the electric motor was a piece of cake. The existing throttle was already electric and so that was easy to adapt to the existing wiring in the powerful electric motor. The brakes needed no alteration.

To charge the battery for the electric motor, he decided to tap into their existing solar array. With a good understanding of electrical systems, he ran wires directly from the solar panels to a dedicated charge controller. The charge controller was simply reprogrammed to charge the 48 volt lithium battery in the ATV. This allowed him to harness the sun's energy and convert it into power for the new electric off-road vehicle. He also added a detachable battery charging plug, making it easy to connect and disconnect the lithium battery for charging. The plug was made from old welding cables that he had laying around, and they were fastened in such a way that you could not accidentally touch the positive and negative together.

The lithium battery itself was a marvel of modern technology, offering high energy density, light weight, and extended lifespan. Jacob calculated that the ATV could travel up to 20 miles on a single charge, a significant improvement over its previous gas-powered range. To further enhance its capabilities, he installed a compact propane generator in the back of the UTV. This generator could be used to charge the battery on the go, effectively extending the vehicle's range and making it a versatile tool for their homestead. Though they rarely used propane, Jacob had a full 1000 gallon propane tank in the back yard, which he had set up to be able to fill smaller tanks as needed. Having a small propane powered generator was a huge capability!

With the conversion complete, the ATV had transformed into a silent, solar-powered workhorse, perfectly suited to the needs of their homestead. Its electric motor provided ample torque for traversing rugged terrain, and its renewable energy source meant that they could operate it without depleting their precious fuel reserves.

Jacob's accomplishment was a testament to his dedication to self-sufficiency and security, as well as a long-term approach to survival. He had turned a long-held dream into a reality, giving their homestead an invaluable tool for years to come.

As the days passed and life settled into a semblance of normalcy on the homestead, Jacob and Ana saw an opportunity to instill valuable life skills in their children. With the absence of traditional school, they embraced the chance to teach their kids the art of homesteading and self-sufficiency.

Emma, at 8 years old, was eager to learn more about the intricacies of animal care. She joined her parents on daily trips to feed and care for the goats and chickens. Under their watchful guidance, she quickly became adept at recognizing signs of health and well-being in their livestock. As it turned colder and they spent more time in the barn, Emma would visit twice per day to make sure that the goats had good hay and water, as well as to check if any of the goats were giving birth or "kidding." Meanwhile, Jacob junior's bond with their loyal Anatolian shepherd guard dog, Max, grew stronger as they patrolled the perimeter together, safeguarding the homestead. Though only 10, little Jake could now be trusted to patrol with an AR-15, out of necessity and for the safety of the family.

As for Ana's sister Mia, at 24 years old, she took charge of preserving the harvested vegetables and meats. Armed with knowledge passed down through generations and the modern techniques she had learned, she pickled, canned, and preserved their bounty to ensure a steady food supply throughout the year. Mia's dedication to preserving their harvest mirrored the skills of her parents far away in Croatia, and her skills were vital to the family's long-term sustainability.

The younger children, Sarah and Michael also played their part in the daily chores. While these twins were too small to handle heavy tasks, they learned by watching and imitating their older siblings. They took pride in helping feed the animals, even if it meant spilling more hay than they gave. They would also help to load small pieces of firewood, and chase the chickens out of their dad's workshop.

Despite the challenges of their situation, Ana dedicated a portion of each day to homeschooling. Their small earth-sheltered home transformed into a classroom, and she tailored lessons to each child's age and learning level. Math, science, history, and reading became an integral part of their daily routine. While they might have been isolated from traditional education, the children were gaining more than just practical knowledge and life skills that would serve them well in the future. She also taught them classes in religion, to arm them spiritually for the possibility of facing hard times, disease, or death.

Times were surprisingly good at the moment on the homestead. They were thriving, but Ana didn't take any of this for granted and she taught the children to rely on their Lord and Creator for strength, just as her parents had taught her. In Croatia, they had faced hunger, the death of loved ones, and tyranny, but they knew that no matter what, the Lord would be their strength and refuge, even in the face of death. She made sure her children were prepared and fortified in the spirit, just as she had been.

Mia would often help with the homeschooling lessons of the children, and one day at the end of lessons, she told the children that she had an announcement. She went over to the old style green chalkboard on the wall and wrote two words, "Baby Rinehart, coming in April," on the board. 8-year-old Emma began jumping up and down excitedly clapping her hands, "Yay, a baby!!," she cheered.

The other children just looked at each other confused, with little Jake, still repeating, "What does that mean, what?" Ana nearly dropped the glass canning jar that she had been cleaning in the next room, as this was just as much of a surprise to her as it was to the children. She immediately went over to her sister and gave her a deep embrace, tears of joy welling up in their eyes. "Yay!," all of the children shouted, with everyone understanding now. "A baby Lion Heart," said little four year old Sarah.

Jacob had been processing meat in the meat grinder and didn't hear a thing, but he and Ana had been suspecting something was new ever since his sister in law arrived. As soon as he saw the writing on the chalk board, he walked up to Mia and gave her a big hug, "Congratulations sister!," he said warmly, "We can't wait for the new addition to the family."

With the news, the family was even more energized than before, and all of their chores took on greater significance, even the children could feel it. The homestead was indeed a hive of activity, with each member of the family contributing their unique strengths. Their days were filled with purpose, hard work and constantly building their self-reliance. As the children grew and learned, they embodied the spirit of homesteading, thriving in a world that demanded adaptability and an unwavering determination.

Chapter 14: Martial law in Marshall

The nearby town of Marshall, once a haven of peace and prosperity, had been thrust into chaos and uncertainty. In the wake of unprecedented events that had shaken the nation, it was now a microcosm of the entire nation. Though Marshall may have at first appeared to be a war-torn region in a far-off land, it was actually the embodiment of the third world in middle of America.

———————

A decade ago, returning from deployments with the U.S. Army, Jacob, had told people that he knew, friends, and family that they should take nothing for granted. "Most people in the world live in poverty," he told them, "If we don't act wisely in this country, if we elect corrupt politicians and if we want to be activists, revolutionaries, and influencers instead of diligent workers, then we will end up like every other failed state." He didn't want it to happen, but it is true that good times make weak men and weak men make bad times. Bad times also make strong men, who in turn, make good times. But the U.S. was clearly at the first and moving to the middle phase of this cycle. This would imply that such cycle could continue on indefinitely but, living in a world of increasingly scarce resources and large nuclear stockpiles, bad times can instead turn into the END OF TIMES.

———————

In Marshall, fall had turned to winter, and winter had turned the situation for locals and refugees from the city into absolute misery. There wasn't enough food to go around, there was still no electricity, and the only way to stay safe was to be armed. Amidst the hardship, a glimmer of hope emerged as the United States military and local emergency services rallied to restore order and basic services to the beleaguered town. The efforts resembled the resilience and determination that had defined the nation in previous times of crisis with one important difference. The difference was that this time martial law had totally replaced the freedoms that Americans had previously cherished. This time, citizens demanded powerful government action to provide security, food, and basic necessities by any means necessary. Most people did not live in the countryside and did not have the knowledge to feed and care for themselves. They knew nothing of self-reliance and therefore demanded that the government provide for them somehow, and the new authoritarian government was attempting to take on that impossible task.

The first order of business was the restoration of law and order. Military personnel, now deployed within the town, patrolled the streets, maintaining a visible presence that deterred criminal elements. Raids were conducted, where marauders and gang members alike were ruthlessly killed and sometimes executed on the spot. Accidents occurred frequently and bystanders were often killed or the wrong house was raided. Hasty burials began to crowd the small city's parks. Curfews were enforced to ensure the safety of residents, and checkpoints were established to monitor movement in and out of the town. Tweakers, or drug users, were beginning to disappear from the landscape. Many had overdosed or died from exposure as the temperature turned cold. Their skinny, gaunt frames and tendency to crash after their drug trips meant that they would fall asleep in sub-zero temperatures and die of hypothermia. The military was also ruthlessly cracking down so many of the drug addicts had been killed in drug raids as well.

With rations running low, some of the soldiers began to engage in illicit activities, confiscating food, and selling it on the black market or trading it for favors from desperate women. The U.S. dollar was almost worthless, with $100 bills being treated like $1's and jewelry or even gold and silver being used as currency. Despite all of this, the residents of Marshall were for the most relieved by the heavy military presence and they felt fortunate to be near the military base. For all of its problems, they considered this arrangement to be a God send compared to the mob rule, and the ruthlessness of gangs and marauders that they had dealt with in the several months since the total collapse.

With order slowly returning, the focus shifted to the restoration of essential services. Electrical power, a lifeline for the community, was gradually brought back online, though intermittently, and only in the town itself. Repair crews were conscripted back into service without pay, and they worked to mend damaged power lines and substations. The hum of generators, a temporary source of electricity, gradually faded as homes and businesses regained access to the grid. Oddly, China had assisted the U.S. military by providing emergency shipments of diesel fuel, power generators, and limited amounts of humanitarian rations. Perhaps this was part of the reason that the U.S. was siding with China amid the growing tensions with India.

Clean water, a precious resource, was restored through a collaborative effort between military engineers and local utilities. Temporary water treatment facilities were set up to purify available water sources, providing many residents with access to safe drinking water, though not in most homes. The sight of residents filling containers at water distribution points was certainly a step in the right direction.

Medical care, always difficult in a time of crisis, was delivered through mobile clinics and field hospitals. Military medical personnel and local healthcare workers worked side by side to treat injuries and illnesses. The wounded were transported to hospitals at the relatively nearby Bullard Air Force Base, for more extensive care.

The delivery of humanitarian aid became a well-coordinated effort. Relief supplies, including food, clean water, and medical provisions, arrived in convoys under military escort. Food distribution centers were established to address the growing issue of hunger. The military, in coordination with relief agencies, delivered very limited rations to the populace, although fights often broke out due to insufficient food supplies.

Refugee camps were re-organized with precision, and with order enforced by the iron fist of the military, provided shelter to those displaced by the chaos. New tents and temporary housing units were erected in an orderly layout, with designated areas for families, medical facilities, and communal kitchens. The military ensured the safety and security of these camps, protecting the vulnerable from potential threats.

Communication systems, vital for coordinating relief efforts, were largely restored, but under total control of the military. Local radio stations broadcasted information on safety measures, aid distribution, as well as updates from government authorities about new laws and regulations. Families separated during the chaos were sometimes able to reconnect through phone services, but these were still not very reliable and there were more days with outages than there were with connectivity.

Citizens of the United States also learned that the civilian government had mostly been suspended, and the Secretary of Defense was to temporarily lead the nation until order was restored. The President of the United States would still assume an important role, primarily dealing with public relations. The U.S. Congress was dismissed until further notice. State and local authorities would now report to military commanders, and the entire United States was now divided into 13 military districts. This would have caused an uproar at any other time in American history but under the current circumstances, citizens were mainly concerned with trying to get food, water, and not freezing to death over the winter.

As days turned into weeks, the town of Marshall teetered on the edge of an uncertain precipice. While the resilience of its residents and the efforts of the military and emergency services provided a glimmer of hope, the specter of hunger loomed large, and despite intermittent electrical restoration, people in certain neighborhoods were reportedly dying by the dozens from exposure and hypothermia as temperatures dipped into the teens. Most of them had no off-grid heat source. Crime was at least held in check by the violent crackdown of the military, but ordinary citizens sometimes felt threatened by the new military overlords. The fragile equilibrium of order and chaos hung in the balance, a testament to the volatile nature of their new dystopian world, where even the most diligent efforts could be shattered at any moment by the capricious forces of an uncertain origin, or even worse, the unflinching laws of nature.

Chapter 15: Orwellian Dawn

In early December, Jacob's neighbor and friend Bill was able to communicate with his buddy the sheriff, who lived on the south side of the town of Marshall on his cattle ranch. Before the arrival of the military, the sheriff and most of his deputies had been "holed up" on the ranch, making brief forays into the town to assist well-armed neighborhood watch groups who maintained order with mixed success. It was the best they could do as they were outnumbered by armed criminal gangs and tweakers by probably at least 200 to 1.

They were relieved when the military finally arrived after 4 months of chaos, and they were basically re-deputized as a paramilitary force under the local military commander, Lieutenant Colonel Swearington, who had been charged with bringing back order to the town of Marshall and the surrounding smaller communities. LTC Swearington had an entire battalion at his disposal, mostly Infantry mounted in old Humvees as well as support personal and one 30-man platoon of military police. The deputies were happy to help but some of them had second thoughts after an incident where an infantry platoon cleared a two story wood-framed apartment building by firing over 1200 rounds from three M240 machine guns from the tops of their Humvees until the building fell silent. The frequent heavy-handed killing of civilians had caused about half of the deputies to defect, most of them living out of town in the countryside.

It was under these circumstances that Bill contacted the Sheriff using their GMRS radios. "How are things in the civilized world Roger?," implored Bill, his curiosity apparent.

The Sheriff replied with an odd seriousness, as if death itself were listening in, "Bill, things are going to get much worse before they get better. Keep your roads blocked as long as you can, but when they come, do not resist the military…"

"Hold up right there!," argued Bill!, "This is America, and I'll be damned if.."

"Bill stop!," interrupted the sheriff, "stop, I don't have time to talk, but this isn't America anymore, you hear me, this is now just another third world country. This military isn't the one that we had before. They are a new generation and were never disciplined, they didn't even get a civics class growing up and their history class was just about how bad America is. Even their English classes were all about trashing this country. Do you think that they care about the constitution or your rights? Besides, they are all half-starved, they have been shot at for months by angry mobs, and they face no consequences for killing civilians. Under orders, they have been confiscating food from all of the farms closer to town, and they are making their way down to you. They are under orders to feed the populated areas at all costs. Hide anything that you don't want them to take. Once they have taken what they can, they will move on."

Bill immediately radioed Jacob to relay the information calling him on the GMRS handheld radio to give him an update. Jacob listened and then offered some insight that he had learned from deployments many years ago to Latin America, Africa, the Middle East, and the Balkans. "Listen Bill," he advised, "it's not like the movies, and you don't want to pretend that you are some rebel force or Mel Gibson in the movie, 'The Patriot.' I've seen the shining path in Colombia and the insurgents in Africa get gunned down and run over by a rag tag government military force with just three machine guns, 10 grenades, and a handful of AK's. Our military is better equipped and they will clear you out with an Apache gunship if you give them an excuse."

"I see what you are saying," replied Bill, "live to fight another day, right?"

"Exactly," said Jacob, "Live to fight another day, my friend. We survived the looters and the marauders, and now we are going to survive this. Now let's get to work hiding our sh**. Oh yeah, and one more thing, you need to go on a diet. They are not going to believe that you don't have any food with those fat squirrel cheeks of yours!" The two men shared one last laugh, and then they got to work preparing for the military's impending arrival.

————————

One gloomy December morning, as the leaves painted the landscape in shades of amber and crimson, the ominous caravan was on the way to Jacob and Ana's homestead. Old military cargo trucks, adorned with cryptic hand-painted insignias, rumbled along the once-peaceful dirt road that led to their haven of self-sufficiency. Machinery could be heard clearing the way, as the military cut and pushed their way through the log obstacles that had stood for months. Two out of six trucks, old green 2 and 1/2 ton cargo trucks, made their way up the steep driveway, halfway up the hill to the Mooreland home, with a dozen ragtag soldiers hopping out and eyeballing the property. The sight was reminiscent of a bygone era, evoking images of Soviet forces confiscating Ukrainian farm products during the famine-riddled 1930s. Fortunately, they had stopped the tucks only halfway up to the home, and the home itself was still out of sight. Instead of the earth-sheltered home, the soldiers surrounded an old RV camper that Jacob had placed there as a decoy. Jacob was between the camper and an old woodshed, tending to a small campfire with some rose hip tea brewing in a small pot. Jacob held his hands up limply, showing that he was unarmed. "Welcome to my home, gentlemen, what's left of it," he said convincingly.

Jacob was met by a grim-faced officer, a captain, who stepped out of the passenger side of one of the trucks, his uniform brimming with badges of authority. His voice, cold and unyielding, carried a stark command as he informed Jacob of the government's demand for their provisions. The captain skipped the introduction, "We don't want any violence, but we are under orders to feed the citizens of this country, and your farm has produced in the past, and it is time you pick up that responsibility again."

Jacob replied meekly, "I'm ex-military, I know the deal captain, and I respect what you are doing. Times have changed, our home and our fields were burned by marauders, our children have succumbed to disease, and my wife and I are just trying to make it through the winter."

"Search the camper!," said the officer coldly as he whispered to his second in command beside him. Ana stepped out of the camper and out of their way. The tranquility that had ruled the homestead for these months was shattered by the implacable force of the state. Nonetheless, Ana and Jacob had come up with a clever ruse. They had set up a mock homestead along their long driveway halfway between the county road and the location of their actual home. The driveway to the top had been blocked and the earth-sheltered home had been camouflaged and concealed. The soldiers believed that they were already at the end of the driveway. The children were with their Aunt Mia, locked inside the saferoom.

The soldiers carried two 5-gallon buckets of half-rotten grain out of the camper, triumphantly, along with two children's coats. "Sir, this is all they have in there," said one of the sergeants. "Load that and the firewood, and we will be on our way," the captain replied tersely. He had probably not expected to find much, and Jacob found a way to meet his low expectations.

In reality, Jacob and Ana Mooreland had put away 5 years of provisions up at their actual home in preparation for any type of catastrophe, including a nuclear winter. Their illusion of starvation and desperation was brilliant and convincing. Both of their faces had been covered in soot, making them appear gaunt and in poor health, and Ana began to sob, hiding her face, as the soldiers loaded all of the firewood.

"Leave a few sticks of wood just for tonight. They have plenty of wood here, we need the rest for the people in the camps," the captain continued, "and I am sorry for your trouble folks but there are people worse off than you. We all have to sacrifice for 'The Greater Good.'"

Jacob replied, feigning desperation, "We won't last the winter captain, could you leave us one bucket of our grain?" Ana just sobbed softly, burying her face in Jacob's shoulder.

The officer, unmoved by his pleas, raised his voice, "Next time, we might have to come inside for dinner; consider yourselves lucky." Jacob nodded in compliance and looked down at the ground as the captain instructed his men to load up into the trucks. After loading up the officer glared at Jacob as they drove away from the homestead. "Get your farm up and running by springtime," he shouted out the window, "for The Greater Good!"

As the military trucks pulled away, Jacob's face relaxed, and he turned to Ana, and said, "enjoy the buckets of maggots captain douche bag."

"Close one," she replied, "you are a genius, I married a genius! The plan worked!" There was no time to chuckle, he called Bill and Scott to warn them of what was coming, though they could surely hear the loud convoy from a mile away.

———————

In the wake of this distressing ordeal, a somber reality settled upon the homestead. They had outwitted the new military government this time, but the idea of unjust confiscation of hard earned provisions left a bitter taste of totalitarianism in its wake, a stark reminder of how the world had devolved into a place where the powerful wielded their authority without empathy or regard for the hardships endured by ordinary citizens.

Jacob's heart ached not only for their loss but also for the countless others all over the nation who were similarly affected. The once-steadfast pillars of their community had been eroded, replaced by a system that prioritized mass confiscation and pillage over opportunity and self-reliance. What incentive would anyone have to produce if this was how they were to be ruled?

———————

After they climbed the hill back to their now well-camouflaged earth-sheltered home, they took care of their chores, feeling a huge, though temporary sense of relief. After another couple of hours, Jacob received a call from Bill. "It worked, thanks for the great idea buddy," Bill told him excitedly. "Just like you said, we burned the old empty hay barn down by the road and concealed the drive up to my house. Then we used Scott's place as the decoy home. They never even realized that my home was up the drive further. They only took some old moldy animal feed and some pots and pans, what an awesome idea you had!"

"I'm glad it worked," replied Jacob, "but soon we will have to come up with a new plan. By early spring, I think the patrols will get more aggressive, and if history is a guide, then the government will likely confiscate land, and probably resettle refugees in the countryside." The men agreed to get together soon, and Jacob settled down for the evening with his family, locked safely in their bunker of a home.

Chapter 16: Doubling Down on Survival

As the days wore on and the memory of the military confiscation still weighed heavily on their minds, Jacob and Ana realized that they needed to take proactive measures to defend what remained of their resources. Sitting idly by was no longer an option. The adults of the family, Jacob, Ana, and Mia, gathered together for a frank discussion about the need to protect what they had left.

"We've got a lot of canned goods and supplies, but we can't afford to have anything else taken from us, the events overseas mean that there still could be a nuclear winter, and our stored supplies would be the only thing keeping us alive," Jacob stated firmly, the gravity of their situation etched into his expression.

Ana nodded in agreement, her eyes reflecting the same determination. "We need to be prepared for the worst. We can't rely on anyone else to protect us."

With a sense of urgency, they set to work. Jacob knew that the key to their defense lay in their ability to protect their home and resources. They spent an entire week training the family on firearms, marksmanship, and tactical maneuvers.

The family assembled their arsenal of weapons, which included rifles, shotguns, and handguns. Jacob and Ana were well-versed in firearm safety and marksmanship, Jacob having grown up in a rural area where hunting was a way of life, and Ana growing up in a Balkan war zone. They were now passing on their knowledge to their children. Mia also needed practice, as she had never been a natural crack shot like her older sister.

Their training sessions were intense and focused. They practiced shooting at targets with precision, honing their marksmanship skills. Ana, with her background in sharpshooting passed down from her father in Croatia, proved to be an excellent teacher. She emphasized the importance of accuracy and control, teaching the two older children to take well-aimed shots rather than spraying bullets indiscriminately. She taught her sister and the children the four fundamentals of marksmanship.

1.Get a steady sight picture, the same sight picture each time.
2.Get a steady position, and she showed them how to fire from the prone, kneeling, standing, and various supported positions.
3.Steady breathing, fire at the natural pauses in your breathing, preferably after exhaling.
4.Trigger squeeze, don't jerk the entire weapon, just make sure the trigger finger only moves straight back and very gently.

They also made sure that all of their weapons were zeroed because a non-zeroed weapon is useless.

Jacob, with an AR-15 rifle in hand, began to explain the intricacies of their arsenal. He held the firearm up for everyone to see, taking his time to break down how it operated. "The AR-15," he explained, "is a semi-automatic rifle, which means that with each pull of the trigger, one round is fired. With iron sites it has an effective range of up to 300 yards, making it ideal for defensive purposes."

Ana chimed in, emphasizing the need for accuracy when firing the AR-15. "Remember," she said, "individual, well-placed shots are more effective than rapid fire. You won't hit anything even close to 300 yards if you don't take time to use the four fundamentals of marksmanship."

Next on the agenda was the .308 sniper rifle. Jacob was well-versed in its operation, having used it for hunting in the past, and even having carried and fired it in combat zones as a young soldier. He set up the weapon on its bipod and began to explain its finer points. The .308 sniper rifle was bolt-action, meaning that after each shot, the shooter had to manually operate the bolt to chamber the next round. This design allowed for greater accuracy. Its effective range was considerably longer than the AR-15, stretching out to around 800 yards, with its variable power scope. He showed everyone how to use and look through the scope. Looking at distant objects through the scope was the children's favorite part. Jacob stressed the importance of stealth and patience when using the sniper rifle. "A well-hidden sniper can change the course of a battle without ever being seen," he remarked.

The family absorbed the lessons, recognizing that their proficiency with these weapons was essential to their defense. Those that were big enough took turns practicing with each firearm, understanding that precision was paramount.

In addition to firearms training, they devoted time to mastering the use of their GMRS radios. They practiced communication protocols and code words, as well as distress signals, ensuring that they could effectively communicate with each other in the event of an emergency or attack. The children were taught how to change the channels on the radio and they practiced memorizing which channels to use to talk internally and also with the neighbors across the valley.

Night vision technology was the next topic of discussion. Jacob had both night vision goggles and infrared lasers, which he believed could provide a significant advantage in low-light situations. This advantage is called a force multiplier, given one man the power of multiple soldiers. He explained how night vision worked, detailing the process of collecting and amplifying ambient light to produce a clear image in near-total darkness. They learned how to adjust the goggles for different lighting conditions and how to avoid sudden flashes of light that could disrupt their night vision. They also practiced walking with the NVG's mounted, which was difficult because with their monocular version, the world seemed 2-dimensional.

Setting up a sniper position was another crucial skill they needed to master. Jacob selected an elevated vantage point on their property and explained the principles of creating an effective sniper nest. He emphasized the importance of cover and concealment, ensuring that the sniper could remain hidden while observing potential threats. They also made "ghillie" suits by taking some old netting and sewing on pieces of burlap and baling twine, as well as natural vegetation. They then sewed this camouflage netting onto some of Jacob's old camouflage uniforms, so that they could wear it. Making a ghillie was actually a fun family activity, especially the part where they practiced hiding and seeing if they could be found.

Throughout the week, they practiced various tactical scenarios. They simulated defending their homestead from different angles, using both the AR-15 and the .308 sniper rifle. Ana offered valuable insights into the art of concealment and patience, while Jacob taught how to assault and counterattack when the enemy was at their weakest, such as when they were reloading or when they had a vulnerability or blind spot.

Their training extended into the night, and the little children were kept inside when it was dark out. The others took turns practicing marksmanship with night vision and infrared lasers. The eerie green glow of the night vision goggles cast an otherworldly hue on their surroundings as they aimed at targets in the darkness. Ana emphasized that using this technology required utmost care, as any lapse in stealth or especially breaking and losing the equipment could lead to dire consequences.

As the next few days of training days passed, the family's proficiency with their weapons and equipment grew exponentially. They had evolved from novices into a well-trained unit, capable of defending their home with precision and skill.

The training had instilled a newfound sense of confidence and unity within the family. They now understood that their survival depended on their ability to protect what was rightfully theirs. Gazing out over their homestead, they were determined to stand their ground and confront whatever challenges lay ahead with unyielding determination.

———————

In the worrisome times that had befallen their community, Jacob continued to keep a vigilant eye on the world through the occasional news updates that he could access via his occasionally functional Starlink Internet connection. The intermittent cell phone service had proved unreliable for staying informed, but the Internet provided a slightly more stable window to the outside world, albeit with its own set of challenges.

What concerned Jacob the most internationally was the increasing tension between the United States and India, two nations that were now edging perilously close to a conflict that had global ramifications. The situation was a geopolitical puzzle, one that seemed to defy reason. The United States had recently redeployed a significant number of troops from their homeland to the Kashmir region of Pakistan, with the stated goal of patrolling the border with India. It was a move that raised eyebrows and sparked debates among international experts.

As the world watched, the United States, under its figurehead, President Williams, made statements of support for Pakistan while urging India to show restraint. President Williams insisted that the deployment was meant to maintain a buffer zone of stability in the region and promote peaceful dialogue between the two nations. However, the news releases from India, voiced by the Indian Prime Minister, took a decidedly different tone. He expressed India's deep concern over what was viewed as an unwarranted military buildup on its borders. He questioned the wisdom of such actions, given India's commitment to a peaceful coexistence in the region and longstanding status as a peaceful democracy. The Indian government called for international mediation to resolve the escalating tensions, emphasizing the need for dialogue and diplomacy.

Simultaneously, the United States, under President Williams' administration, was pursuing a series of surprising deals with China. The Chinese Communist Party (CCP), had inked agreements to supply vast amounts of agricultural products to the United States. It was an unprecedented move that left many baffled, considering the relatively recent history of tensions between the two nations.

The news reports were filled with debates and speculations on the motives behind these unusual developments. It was most likely that the United States was making strategic concessions to the CCP in a bid to secure its aid and support after the American economy had collapsed. It was also clear that the United States was no longer in a position to call the shots. They were desperate to receive food and agricultural shipments from China, and the U.S. servicemembers deployed to Kashmir were likely a bargaining chip in this negotiation.

To Jacob, a well-read history major, this was a clear sign of the development of the U.S. as a new vassal state. The collapse of the American economy left the U.S. government decapitated. President Williams was a figurehead who would kowtow to the CCP and China would use the U.S. to do its dirty work as a proxy against their rival, India. It was empire-building 101 and China was playing three dimensional chess. A great number of military officers in the American military were clearly compromised as well, as they had been making inexplicable pro-Chinese statements in public for years. In the increasingly murky backwater area north of Richmond, Virgina, the top level brass at the pentagon had even started to take direct bribes from the CCP.

While the rest of the country burned in riots, the capitol area flourished; this included a wide area around D.C., Alexandria, the Pentagon, and even farther north into Montgomery County, Maryland. There had never been a security lapse in these areas, and lavish goods from overseas and especially China kept the families of America's government elite, well-fed and even living lives of excess. The capitol was the lap of luxury, increasingly controlled and funded by the Chinese Communist Party. The rest of the country had been turned into mere military districts to be administered by the corrupt and comprised U.S. government elite, and their defense department cronies and henchmen. This system was designed primarily to enrich China in the years to come, and harness America's resources, redirecting them to supply and feed the massive and hungry Chinese population. The crony government in D.C. was now only serving to facilitate this transfer of wealth and resources.

For Jacob and Ana, the unfolding global drama added another layer of uncertainty to their already precarious situation. They couldn't help but wonder how these international events might ripple down to their remote homestead. In a world where alliances were shifting, and once-stable relationships were unraveling, they found themselves more isolated than ever, relying on their own resilience and resourcefulness to navigate the uncertain path that lay ahead.

Jacob's sister-in-law, Mia, began to feel an overwhelming anxiety that had grown with each passing day, a heavy burden that weighed on her heart. Her husband, an Air Force pilot, had been deployed to a destination shrouded in secrecy, and communication with him had become sporadic, at best. Her biggest fear was that her unborn child would never meet its father. The uncertainty gnawed at her, leaving her sleepless and consumed by worry.

By day, as she looked out over the forested hills of the homestead, Mia couldn't shake the feeling of helplessness that had settled upon her. She longed for the familiar sound of her husband's voice, for the reassurance of his presence, but all she had were fleeting and vague messages that provided little insight into his whereabouts or mission. The military's new encrypted e-mail system was censored and regulated by AI, in order to filter out potential risks to operational security. This made it cumbersome and unreliable.

The strain of waiting and worrying took a toll on Mia, affecting not only her emotional well-being but also her interactions with the children. She was increasingly distant and careless with them. On one occasion, while mentally distracted, she let the 4 year old twins walk down the driveway halfway to the county road by themselves. Now Ana could barely trust her to watch the children anymore. Mia yearned for the day when her husband would return, when they could embrace without the shadow of uncertainty looming over them. Until then, she clung to the hope that he would come home safe and sound, and that their family would be reunited once more.

As the New Year came and went, and on through the dark evening hours of February, Jacob, Ana, and Mia found themselves increasingly absorbed in discussions about the changing world order and its potential consequences. By day, they continued to put away food, ensure their water tanks were topped off, and that their perimeter was secure. They also attempted to camouflage as much of their buildings from the air as possible. The safety of their family and especially the children was the most important thing in their lives, and they grappled with the uncertainty of what lay ahead. The one thing they could be certain of was the need to remain vigilant and prepared for even the worst imaginable scenarios that the future might bring. It's better to be prepared for a disaster that never comes than to fail to prepare and then it strikes!

Chapter 17: Who Are the Good Guys?

It was a cloudy afternoon when young Tommy, the 8 year old son of their neighbor Scott, came running up the hill to Jacob and Ana's homestead. He was visibly exhausted and drained; his face was white, as if completely drained of blood, and was etched with a mixture of fear, grief, and disbelief. He was barely able to catch his breath as he began to recount a harrowing tale that would send shockwaves through the community.

"Mr. Jacob! Mrs. Ana!" Tommy gasped, his voice trembling. "You won't believe what happened at Grandpa Bill's house! They came... the government forces... and..."

Jacob and Ana exchanged worried glances, their hearts sinking as they sensed the gravity of Tommy's words. They had long feared that the ever-expanding government presence could spell trouble for their peaceful neighborhood community.

"Slow down, Tommy," Jacob urged gently. "Take a deep breath and tell us what happened."

Tommy nodded and took a moment to compose himself before he continued, his voice quivering with emotion. "They came in the morning, Mr. Jacob. There were trucks and soldiers everywhere. They said they were looking for criminals, but... but, no criminals, it wasn't like that, they are bad soldiers, bad guys," he began to cry.

As Tommy recounted the events, it became clear that what had transpired was nothing short of a nightmare. Government forces had descended upon Bill's house with overwhelming firepower, their actions swift and ruthless. Tommy's eyes welled up with tears as he described how the soldiers had stormed the property, shouting orders and demanding information.

"They asked about anyone suspicious," Tommy said, his voice cracking. "But before anyone could say anything, they just... they just started shooting."

The horror of the situation began to sink in for Jacob and Ana. Bill, a friend and neighbor, had always been a pillar of their community. Scott himself had served his country in a law enforcement role, and had been part of more just times. Jacob regarded both of them with fondness, recognizing their generosity and willingness to help others in times of need. Their entire families were an example of what was right in the world. It was inconceivable that they could be gunned down by their own government.

"Did your grandpa and your family...?" Ana's voice trailed off, unable to finish the sentence.

Tommy nodded, tears streaming down his face. "Yes, Mrs. Ana. They... they didn't make it. Mom and Dad, Grandma and Grandpa... they're all gone." The boy seemed broken inside but strangely hardened on the surface. It was as if the child had been murdered but a tough and old façade had replaced the face of what was once a sweet and innocent child. His eyes were glazed over, pupils were large, skin was clammy and dirty, hair was matted. Part of the human had died in him, and the beast inside was growing, even inside of the boy.

Jacob's heart ached as he contemplated the devastating loss. Bill's house, once a place of warmth and camaraderie, was another casualty in the destruction of America, consumed by the advent of this new Dark Age.

"Did they say why they did this, Tommy?" Jacob asked, his voice trembling with a mixture of anger and sorrow.

Tommy nodded again, his words heavy with sorrow. "They said it was for the "Greater Good," that they were protecting us from criminals. But... but they didn't listen. They didn't care, there's no good, just death, everybody's dead!"

The chilling reality that unfolded before them raised unsettling questions about the intentions of the government forces. The military, once a source of security, now appeared as a clear threat to the very community it was meant to protect.

As Tommy's story continued, he described how the soldiers had ransacked their homes, belongings, and provisions, leaving them with nothing but the clothes on their backs.

Jacob and Ana listened intently; their hearts pained with a growing sense of dread. The innocence of their idyllic community had been shattered, replaced by a haunting uncertainty. They realized that in a world where trust had eroded, it was increasingly challenging to discern who the real "good guys" were and what the future held for their once-peaceful enclave.

As Tommy grew silent, Ana took him to get some food as the other children stared. They wanted to play but could sense that it was not yet the time for play. They were patient and they could feel empathy for the boy, especially Little Jake, who was only one year older than Tommy. Jake desperately wanted to be the boy's friend, and while he could sense a deep, terrible sadness in Tommy, he hoped that in time, the boy would feel happy again, and they could play like normal boys, in a normal world.

Jacob, whispered something to Ana and he slipped out of the home quickly, slinging his Ar-15 and grabbing his chainsaw on the way out. "Little Jake," he called back down the stairs. "Little Jake grab the other AR-15, I need you to just pull security for me while I cut some trees. "Roger that dad!," responded Jake proudly. For the first time that day, Tommy looked at the older boy as Jake climbed the stairs with the sniper rifle on his shoulder. It was the first of many times that he would look up to and feel the urge to emulate the boy who would soon become like a brother to him.

Jacob and his son Jake headed down to the county road, and began cutting trees to drop them across and block the route heading in the direction of Bill and Scott's homes. With the Harris family gone, victims to America's new brutal third world military, Jacob and his family were on their own. He had already dropped trees in the direction of Highway 77, but somehow the military had approached Bill's home from the other direction. The easiest thing to do was use the fallen trees to barricade themselves from that backroad in case the soldiers decided to return. It wouldn't hold the soldiers off indefinitely but at least it would slow them down and give the family more time to prepare. Little Jake took up a position on the ridge just above his father as Jacob cut the trees, looking out for any danger, soldiers, criminals, or marauders, as his father worked.

Just as Jacob finished felling the last tree, he looked up at Tommy, who was pointing frantically at a tree line along the road, behind Jacob and on the opposite side from Jake. It was a blind spot and Jacob knew that if someone were to surprise him, then that would be where they would come from. Without having time to unsling his rifle, Jacob spun and looked up at the steep embankment on the side of the road, into the thick tree line. There he saw Lester Cutshall, staring back down at him, only 50 feet away, with a small rifle, a .243 at the low ready, pointing at the ground. It would have been unwise for Jacob to escalate the situation by unslinging his own rifle.

Lester was almost unrecognizably skinny, pale, with hollow cheeks and a completely bald head. Jacob could still recognize the criminal because of his thick forehead and bushy eyebrows that grew together above his crooked nose; a nose flattened from years of fist fights, brawls, and altercations that Lester loved to instigate. His head had not been shaved but instead his hair had clearly fallen out from using the drug Ultraquin. For being a tweaker and user of the powerful stimulant, Lester was remarkably calm, and talked slow, in a lazy southern accent and oddly high-pitched, nasally voice.

"That boy up on that ridge belong to you?," asked Lester.

Jacob was not intimidated and replied calmly, "He does, and he's a real shooter so you might not want to raise that rifle."

"I wasn't!," snapped Lester, with a hard stare, "I's just looking for Jesse, you seen my brother 'round here?," he asked, calming back down.

"I seen him before Marshall burned last fall," Jacob replied convincingly, "He was in that yellow and black Mustang up on highway 77, I think that car belonged to his girlfriend's parents, didn't it."

"Yeah, but they dead now," responded Lester, strangely defensive. "Trisha's with me now, she's my woman, my brother disappeared so I look after her until Jesse comes home."

Jacob was contemplating unslinging his rifle but he knew it would be unwise. At least Lester was on the defensive now. "I'll keep an eye out for your brother," said Jacob, and then asked, "You seen the Army 'round here?"

"Oh, they around," said Lester matter-of-factly, and they ain't all bad, I got friends you know, I'll be seeing you then," he said, with a slight, backing into the forest and keeping his eye on Jacob until he was out of sight. Jacob quickly unslung his AR-15, leaped out of the roadway and up the steep embankment, quickly scanning and taking aim. But it was too late, Lester knew who he was dealing with and had begun running immediately, around the bend, back down to the creek and out of sight, towards his old homeplace, which was far on the other side of the Harris property.

The Cutshall place had been burned down, presumably by Scott, when the collapse first started. It wasn't much to begin with, just an old trashy trailer beside an even older farmhouse that was uninhabitable. It was more of a hideout for criminals than a home. After Scott had burned it, they all hoped that the Cutshalls would never come back. Their father had died many years ago from an overdose and the mother had been shacked up with a mean, ugly drug dealer with an illegal chop shop, halfway towards the town of Marshall, on highway 77. Jacob had hoped that Lester would stay up there. He knew that the criminal, a 25 year old with arrested mental development, loved to be close to town where he maintained a lot of gang connections and could always get a resupply of his new favorite drug, ultraquin.

It was a shame that Lester had escaped, but he had approached Jacob at a vulnerable moment and Jacob had been lucky that Lester had not fired. It had been a wise move to have little Jake providing security, even just as a deterrent. There was no way that Jacob was going to pursue Lester at this point and leave his son there all alone, and the boy wasn't ready to follow him and hunt down a criminal. He was too young for that. The boy had performed well, and it was going to be a good lesson for him in the long run. Unfortunately, they now had one more thing to worry about and Jacob wondered just how deep of a connection Lester had with the soldiers in their area. That was truly a disturbing thought. Jacob and his son had finished the new roadblocks and headed back up to the homestead to share the news with Ana.

———————

Back at their home, and with the grim tale of his family etched in his mind, Tommy found solace and comfort in the presence of Ana, Mia and the children. Over the following weeks, he became a part of their family, seeking refuge not only from the harsh realities of the world outside but also from the haunting memories of that fateful day. Ana, with her nurturing warmth, provided the motherly care Tommy desperately needed, while the other children embraced him as a new friend and playmate, a sibling even.

Being just a little younger than Jacob junior, he soon began following and imitating the older boy. They taught him the rules of gun safety and how to hunt so that he could help provide for the family. The family ate a lot of squirrels and occasionally racoons that were hunted by the boys. The racoons were especially valuable as a source of fat and lard for cooking. The young hunters also kept the chickens and the family dog, Max, well-fed during the dark days of the long winter.

———————

During the long dark winter nights, Jacob was able to occasionally monitor the international military situation through his government-linked GIS program and he couldn't help but feel a growing sense of unease. The troop movements he had witnessed on the screen seemed to align with the reports he had read earlier. The United States was indeed redeploying its forces, not only within its own territory but also where they would directly threaten India, possibly doing China's bidding.

Publicly, the government's focus had shifted from military operations overseas to internal security and rebuilding, but on the top secret side of things that Jacob had access to with the GIS, American defense hardware was focused squarely on the Indian Ocean, and all around India.

What concerned Jacob even more were clues regarding China's activities in the Pacific. Occasionally there were estimated locations of foreign units on the GIS program monitored by Jacob. These reports painted a picture of a region in grave danger, as there were indications that China had begun stationing troops in locations closer to Hawaii and the U.S. mainland. The precise reasons behind these deployments remained shrouded in secrecy, and in the sparse news reports on the internet, the international community was silent on China's intentions.

One report indicated that China had established a military presence on a small uninhabited island in the Pacific, belonging to the Philippines, raising alarm among neighboring nations. The Philippines was in no position to counter the move without U.S. help. The U.S. government issued statements expressing concern over these developments, urging a peaceful resolution to the growing tensions. However, as Jacob delved deeper into the GIS program's data, he knew that these diplomatic efforts were a mere smoke screen. The troop movements said one thing, and the politicians would say something completely different.

International troop movements were not limited to the Pacific or U.S. so-called "peacekeeping" efforts in Pakistan. Reports also emerged of increased military activity along the border between India and China, further fueling tensions between the two nations. The situation was reminiscent of past border disputes, but this time, the stakes seemed higher, with both sides unwilling to back down.

As Jacob continued to gather information, he discovered that the U.S. government had initiated diplomatic talks with India and China, urging restraint and peaceful negotiations. The world watched anxiously, hoping that a peaceful resolution could be reached to avert a potential military clash.

In addition to these developments, China had become a close ally of Australia within a very short time frame, less than a year. China even opened a new military base at a leased port in Australia, significantly expanding their presence in the region. The base was reportedly well-fortified and equipped to handle a large contingent of troops.

As tensions continued to mount, Jacob couldn't help but wonder about the naval power China had amassed in the Pacific. Reports indicated that the Chinese Navy had deployed a variety of vessels, including aircraft carriers, destroyers, and submarines. Their naval presence in the region had grown exponentially, and this buildup seemed to have the potential to dominate the entire Pacific any time the Chinese military was given the order.

Chinese naval vessels dominated the South China Sea and conducted exercises in disputed waters, leading to increased friction with neighboring countries, especially the Philippines. The situation at sea had become increasingly complex, with potential flashpoints that could escalate into international conflicts at any moment.

––––––––––––

Meanwhile on the homestead, Jacob knew that there was no time to be complacent. Geopolitical events were moving so quickly that he knew that extreme consequences could not be ruled out and he did not want to be taken by surprise in the event of an EMP (electromagnetic pulse) weapon, use of nuclear weapons, or by the tsunamis of ripple effects that could emanate from this geopolitical power struggle.

As winter began to further tighten its grip on the land in late February, Jacob felt the weight of responsibility pressing down upon him. The snow-covered landscape added an air of serenity to their homestead, but it also brought a sense of dread and urgency. With their supplies now more limited, he knew he had to venture into the forest to secure additional sustenance for his family.

One cold morning, as the first rays of dawn painted the sky with hues of pink and gold, Jacob set out on his hunt. He carried his trusty .308 sniper rifle, the weapon he had trained with rigorously over the past weeks, and identical to the one that he had carried on combat deployments many years ago, when he was still proud of what his country was doing. Clad in winter gear and moving with practiced stealth, he followed the well-worn deer paths through the dense woods.

The forest seemed eerily silent, as if it held its breath in anticipation. Jacob's senses were heightened, his every step calculated. He had spent years learning the art of hunting, and this day was no different, or so he thought.

As he approached a clearing, he noticed movement in the distance, a mere 100 yards—a shadowy figure, crouched low, seemingly focused on something ahead. Instinctively, Jacob dropped to one knee, his finger lightly resting on the trigger. He peered through his scope, adjusting the magnification to get a better look.

Through the crosshairs of his scope, Jacob could now make out the poacher's profile. The man was clad in rugged attire, his face obscured by a tattered scarf. He appeared to be armed, a rifle slung across his shoulder. The sight sent a shiver down Jacob's spine; this was a confrontation he hadn't anticipated.

Jacob tried to discern the poacher's intentions, and if he was alone, he spotted movement from the man—a reflection, the glint of sunlight reflecting off metal. Panic surged through him as he realized the poacher had raised his own rifle. In the span of heartbeats, their eyes locked, and a deadly game of miscommunication and confusion unfolded.

In the breathless silence of the forest, the first shot rang out—a deafening crack that reverberated through the trees. Jacob's training kicked in, and he instinctively returned fire, the round from his .308 rifle cracking through the trees and striking the warm flesh of the man's chest. The man thrashed and choked, and Jacob could hear the gurgling sounds as the poacher drowned on his own blood and on the shattered tissue from his lungs in a painful but futile struggle.

After a few moments, the poacher was still, motionless on the ground, and visible in the distance through Jacob's sights. Jacob quickly closed the gap to his unexpected foe.

Upon arrival, he found himself torn between relief and remorse. Jacob stood there, his thoughts a confused combination of conflicting emotions. A stranger, the fallen poacher's eyes were already glazed over in the cold, his breathing had not completely stopped but was extremely shallow, and life had all but slipped away from him. The snow was red in a widening circle beneath the man, and his chin was covered with warm frothy crimson blood and bits of lung tissue. After one more last strained wheeze from the dying man, the silence once again settled over the wood, broken only by the distant chatter of crows and the rustling of leaves in the cold breeze. It was as if the peace of the forest had never been broken.

Jacob's mind raced as he contemplated his next move. The world had become a shadow of its former self, and the old rules no longer applied. The once-reliable institutions were gone and asking for outside help was out of the question, a thing of the past.

Reluctantly, Jacob made a pragmatic decision. He searched his memory and remembered a nearby drainage ditch that he had dug with a backhoe years ago, one of the many preparations he had made for the uncertainties of the future.

Determined but burdened by the grim task at hand, Jacob began to drag the lifeless body towards the ditch. The forest seemed to close in around him, as if nature itself was consulting with Jacob about the morality of this somber act. The poacher, once a threat, now lay still, and his secrets needed to be buried with him.

Jacob began dragging the man, and with each step, his mind raced with thoughts of survival, the desperate measures he was willing to take to protect his family. He lowered the poacher into the trench, careful to conceal the lifeless form beneath the cold earth. He pushed and scraped with a large branch as frozen soil and moss fell in heavy clumps, covering the truth of that fateful encounter. The bloody trail would be impossible to erase and he would rely on nature and the continuing snowfall to conceal it for him.

As he stood there, sweat mingling with the cold chill of the forest, Jacob knew that he had taken a step into an uncertain darkness. Though he felt justified, the decision weighed on his conscience, but in this new dark world, trust had become a rare commodity, and survival demanded unorthodox choices. He wondered how many men his ancestors had to put beneath the dirt in order to survive over the hard and dark centuries of human history. Darkness and struggle had certainly been the rule and not the exception.

With the deed done, Jacob turned away from the makeshift grave, his resolve steeled. He knew that the world beyond the forest had become a perilous and unpredictable place. In the eerie silence of the woods, he could only hope that he had made the right choice—one that would safeguard his family and prevent at least this poacher from taking any more of their food supply, though he was sure that others would follow.

As he traveled back home through the dense woods, Jacob couldn't shake the fear that morality was being sacrificed in this new dark age, where survival seemed to eclipse all other concerns. He thought about the old days, when they had followed the rules of society, cherished principles like honesty, charity, trust, and compassion. But now, those ideals were overshadowed by the pressing need to protect his family, to ensure their very existence from one day to the next. It was a different mindset and those that failed to adapt would perish. "Kill or be killed."

———

Arriving back at the homestead, Jacob barely had a chance to catch his breath before Ana approached with a grave expression. He instantly resolved not to share what had happened between himself and the poacher. She held a tablet connected to their Starlink Internet, and her voice was strained as she began to share the news that had just come in. Jacob's heart sank further as he braced himself for the ominous report.

For the next harrowing hours, Jacob and Ana huddled together, dissecting the alarming news reports that streamed in through their suddenly functioning Starlink connection. From the news reports, the world seemed to be unraveling at an alarming pace, with open warfare erupting in South Asia. Their already precarious hope for a normal future was crumbling, replaced by the unpredictable chaos of a world turned upside down.

Early reports indicated that American forces were fighting alongside Pakistanis against the Indians in the contested region of Kashmir. Bombers from the American military had commenced devastating runs on Indian cities from the strategic base on the island of Diego Garcia, an act that plunged the region into turmoil. In a grim twist of fate, Chinese forces had also entered the fray, attacking India from the opposite side, and seizing large areas of territory near the Indian-controlled Himalayan mountains and rolling through Nepal unopposed. Bangladesh had been a rival of India since its inception, though never strong enough to assert itself. Now, they were deeply emboldened, and the crowded citizens of Bangladesh were seen in videos toppling the border fences in the areas of Assam and east of Calcutta, while a motley crew of civilians mixed with Bangladeshi soldiers commandeered Indian farms and villages along the border regions.

This was not a war for oil or minerals. Instead, agricultural land and access to rivers of freshwater were what nation states now prized above all else. In the old world order, energy sources, diesel fuel, and manufacturing were horded by the powers that be. In this newly emerged world order, it was clear that energy and fuel were becoming less necessary. With their booming populations, countries like, India, Pakistan, China, and Bangladesh could easily afford to expend people, using their bodies and their labor to power their national ambitions.

Jacob and Ana listened in disbelief as the reports detailed the escalating violence, the suffering of countless innocents caught in the crossfire, and the geopolitical tensions that threatened to plunge their world into even greater turmoil.

As they absorbed the gravity of the situation, the homestead around them felt like a small island of stability in an increasingly turbulent sea. In the midst of it all, they clung to one another, their family, in the hope that somehow, they would find a way to navigate the treacherous path ahead by closing out the outside world and becoming increasingly self-reliant.

Chapter 18: Prepare for the Worst

As Jacob and Ana huddled in the dimly lit kitchen, their faces etched with concern, the gravity of their situation weighed heavily upon them. The news from the Starlink Internet had been nothing short of catastrophic, and Jacob couldn't shake the growing fear that a nuclear conflict loomed on the horizon.

"Ana," he began solemnly, "we need to prepare for the worst. I believe that nuclear war is imminent, it's only a matter of time. With tensions escalating between superpowers like the United States, India, and China, one of these countries will be the first, but not the last to use nuclear weapons in this conflict. If retaliatory nuclear strikes begin, they could end up causing a nuclear winter, which is the most difficult situation to prepare for, even here on our remote homestead."

Ana's eyes filled with apprehension as she nodded in agreement. "You're right, Jacob. We can't afford to be complacent. We've come this far, and we won't let everything we've done be for nothing. We have made so many preparations and we need to finish the job and top everything off so that our efforts are not wasted."

―――――――――

Their first order of business was to ensure that their water supply remained uncontaminated. With diligent care, they filled and covered some additional large water storage tanks located near the barn, shielding them from potential fallout. They had a concrete cistern already, but filling the water-hauling tanks that they had used for livestock would be a great additional source. While these poly-tanks had secure lids and were now mostly buried, they had also been used for rainwater collection. The rainwater spouts were sealed and the tanks were covered with two layers of 12 mil plastic and sandbags to ensure that no nuclear fallout would contaminate them. Luckily, Jacob had purchased stacks of empty sandbags prior to the collapse. They had filled most of them from the sand in their creek and now had an excellent stockpile. This water along with the water in the concrete cistern, would need to be treated about once every 6 weeks by adding ¼ cup of hypochlorite for every 500 gallons. It could not be drunk for 48 hours after adding this treatment. The hypochlorite was an item that could be sealed and stored indefinitely in a dry area. It had to be kept far from living quarters in order to prevent possible but unlikely explosions from the gases. Pre-collapse, it had been relatively cheap and so now that it was valuable, the Mooreland family was sitting on a virtual goldmine of hypochlorite with nearly endless water purification potential.

Next, they turned their attention to the safe room, a reinforced chamber that was built inside and as a part of their earth-sheltered home and was designed to shield them from nuclear radiation and fallout. They meticulously checked the functionality of the air filtration system, making sure it was in optimal working condition. It had been a costly investment, but one that could prove invaluable in the event of a nuclear emergency.

The safe room filtration system drew air from a pipe that went directly above ground so as not to unnecessarily pull air into the house or the rear escape tunnel. The charcoal air filter was in a very secure hidden metal container on the surface of the ground, and it had a dual air pumping system. One method of pumping was a modified hand-cranked blacksmith forge pump, and the other was a 4 inch, 12 volt inline pipe fan. In the case that the 12 volt solar batteries failed, they could bring filtered air into the safe room with the hand crank pump. If the room had to be sealed, it would not have to be cranked 24-7, just 5-6 times per day, for about 15 minutes each time. A nuclear catastrophe was unthinkable to most people, but for Jacob, unthinkable did not mean impossible, and it was something that he had planned for during the construction of their home.

Their food stores were another critical concern. They had accumulated a vast stockpile over the years, consisting of canned goods, grains, dehydrated vegetables, and more. As Ana assessed their supplies, she made a meticulous inventory, noting expiration dates and putting items that had almost reached their shelf life up front so that they could be consumed first.

"We can't afford to run out of essentials," Ana remarked, her voice tinged with determination. "We'll need to ration our food carefully and ensure we have enough to last us through a protracted crisis."

Jacob nodded in agreement, a sense of responsibility weighing heavily on his shoulders. "We have to be prepared for the long haul, Ana. It's not just us; it's the kids, too. We owe it to them to keep them safe, secure, and in a healthy mental state."

With their preparations in full swing, they discussed contingency plans and protocols with their children. They kept plenty of books for children of all ages in the safe room, along with board games, in case they had to be locked down for a long period of time. The older ones were old enough to understand the gravity of the situation, and they shared in the responsibility of maintaining the family's well-being.

"Jacob," Ana said softly as they paused to catch their breath, "I can't help but think about Tommy. He's been through so much already, and now this."

Jacob sighed, feeling a deep concern for the young boy they had taken under their wing. "We'll do our best for him, just like we will for our own. Little Jake has really taken him in and treated him like a brother, and I am going to include both of the boys on projects that we need to do around the homestead. We will start by butchering as many goats as we have room to store meat for."

With a renewed sense of purpose, they continued their preparations, hoping against hope that their worst fears would never come to pass. But they understood that in these uncertain times, being ready for anything was the only way to ensure their family's survival.

———————

As the days wore on, Jacob and Ana continued to monitor the bleak news updates pouring in through their Starlink Internet connection. The world was embroiled in a tumultuous conflict, and each piece of news brought fresh waves of distress.

The war, which had erupted in the heart of the Indian subcontinent, showed no signs of abating. The conflict was now more clearly divided into two opposing forces, with India and its ally, Russia, facing off against Pakistan and the United States. Russia, oddly enough, had been a close ally of China, but now was providing material and air support to India, but only directly targeted Pakistan and nearby U.S. targets, never China. Were they possibly somehow doing China's bidding? The once peaceful regions were now battlegrounds, and casualties mounted daily.

Pakistan, bolstered by American support, had unleashed its military might in the disputed Kashmir region, causing immense suffering to the local population. News reports spoke of villages reduced to rubble and countless civilians caught in the crossfire. This was sixth generation warfare, and both sides were using civilians as human shields and as propaganda to make the other side look like butchers. Asymmetrical fighters in civilian clothes were abundant on both sides and made use of drones, improvised explosive devices, and even powerful blinding lasers to make the front line a literal meat grinder.

China, seizing the opportunity presented by the chaos, had launched a massive offensive along the northern border of India. Their well-coordinated assault aimed at securing vast swathes of territory, and it was evident they were making significant gains. Indian cities lay in ruins as they faced the onslaught of the formidable Chinese military machine. The only thing that stabilized the front line and stopped India from being overrun was the fact that they had 1.5 billion citizens, half of whom were eligible to be drafted, and fed into the grinder for potentially years to come.

Amidst the military strife, civilian casualties reached staggering numbers. Images of displaced families, with gruesome wounds, fleeing their homes with nothing but the clothes on their backs were shocking to Jacob and Ana, even compared to what they had seen in their own country. The specter of human suffering was a stark reminder of the world's descent into madness.

"The situation is worse than I expected, it makes living here seem idyllic, even with our huge problems," Ana remarked to her husband. "The civilian population is bearing the brunt of this conflict, and with both sides being nuclear armed it's only a matter of time before either India or Pakistan drops a nuke."

Jacob nodded grimly, and she knew he was serious and determined to survive anything, even a nuclear apocalypse. "We're fortunate to be away from the epicenter of this turmoil, but there is a huge danger that it will spill over. There are too many nuclear-armed countries involved; the U.S., China, India, Pakistan, and Russia all have nukes. One country could use a nuke and credibly blame another country."

As they discussed the ongoing strife, their thoughts inevitably turned to Mia's husband, a military officer whose whereabouts and mission remained shrouded in secrecy. The uncertainty gnawed at them, and they yearned for a glimmer of hope or a message from the conflict zone, letting them know he was okay. Mia was so visibly worried that it was not even possible to speak to her about the situation; she just could not handle it. She spent most of her time now working on puzzles or artwork, just to keep her mind off of the situation. The children had always loved their Aunt Mia and they helped her stay calm and tranquil more than anything else.

Through it all, their homestead remained an island of relative peace, but they knew that the turbulent world beyond their borders meant that vigilance had to be maintained.

Chapter 19: Bombing Runs

Major Mark Rinehart had been deployed for 6 months in a war zone, in an experience that had turned out to be both harrowing and dull, terrifying and comfortable, unsettling and inspiring. Mark's squadron was not even designed to be deployed. Being a pilot of the new B-21 Raider meant that you would never expect to be deployed. Originally all of their missions were meant to be flown from Bullard Air Force Base in Arkansas, so that the highly classified top secret design and nature of the Air Force's most advanced strategic bomber would never come close to the enemy's prying eyes. The Aircraft could easily cruise at 600 miles per hour and had the most advanced stealth technology known to man, so there was no need to plant it at some base overseas, it could do everything it needed to do and fly right back to Arkansas.

For this reason, Mark and the rest of his squadron was both surprised and unsettled to find that they would be deploying last fall, and now that it was March, they were growing desperate for some explanation of why they were still on the atoll of Diego Garcia, and why they had been conducting bombing runs against a former ally, the nation of India. It was indeed an experience with extreme highs and extreme lows for Mark, constant emotional ups and downs as Mark flew terrifying missions high over futuristic warzones where nations whose Armies numbered in the millions simultaneously fed battalions, regiments, and entire divisions into a meat grinder. Though Mark always flew high above the fray in the dark of the night, the size of the battlefront along the India-Pakistan Border was so huge that he could witness miles and miles of burning fields, buildings, and vehicles, as constant streams of tracers flew into the night sky, far below his flight altitude.

The technology on the aircraft was such that all of his targets were pre-programmed and it was very easy for him to monitor the onboard systems with ease while spending most of his time scanning for threats. The integrated AI of his B-21 knew the mission, and made most of the decisions for the pilot, with Major Rinehart simply giving the final okay to launch munitions or alter their flight path. There were multiple occasions where Mark had been alerted by the AI that enemy aircraft were in the area, to include India's own HAL Tejas multirole fighter and it's Mi-35 attack helicopters. The auxiliary bays of the B-21 carried the most advanced air-to-air missiles known to man that with a push of a button, Mark had launched frequently and with ease to vaporize the enemy aircraft. While Mark loved the feeling of flying and marveled at the technology that he was privileged enough to harness, he couldn't help wondering why he was ordered to unleash so much destruction on India, a country that had been seen as an ally, and the world's largest Democracy, for as long as Mark had been alive.

Unlike previous conflicts, it seemed that military commanders were acting more as paid mercenaries and took little time to inspire their men by explaining the significance and importance of their mission. Mark also knew that while he was on the western front along Pakistan, China had also been fighting along the northern front. He couldn't help but wonder if his orders were actually handed down from Beijing, through duplicitous forces and traitors working in the pentagon and the white house. His sense of duty and patriotism was such that he instinctually obeyed and almost never questioned orders, but over the last few months, he was having trouble making sense of the world.

Mark found the job of being a pilot of the worlds most advanced aircraft to be both morally disturbing and oddly comfortable, and there was the strange sensation that he was playing at being a god. At the same time, he was deeply conflicted inside, and often had terrifying nightmares that he was actually on the ground, observing things as a ground combatant.

In his dreams there would be screams of pain, dead civilians, and burning buildings. The dream always ended with the streak of a missile across the sky towards his position on the ground, and he would awaken, drenched in sweat. Being an officer, his quarters were more than adequate, with an incredible view of the Indian Ocean. After awaking from his terrible nightmares, he would often open his window and let the warm ocean air dry the cold sweat from his body.

Occasionally after these terrible dreams, Mark would walk down to the sandy beach, wade out into the warm tropical waters, and go for a short swim. He was losing sleep either way, and this was better than lying in bed, tossing back and forth going over moral dilemmas or drifting back into more terrible dreams of death and destruction. Besides, the night air on Diego Garcia was warm, and he felt closer to God when he was bathing in the warm currents, gazing up at bright stars on one of the loveliest parts of all creation in the middle of the Indian Ocean.

Mark would marvel at how the anti-missile and anti-aircraft systems on Diego Garcia and the surrounding naval vessels had kept their base completely safe for these many months. At the same time, all of the wonderful military technology that protected them could not help him establish reliable communication to his wife back home. He had very rarely been able to reach his beloved wife, and when he did it was only through very brief e-mail messages consisting of data bursts that were vetted and chopped up by AI technology in order to prevent the leaking of classified material. All of the communication had been through his military e-mail account and the sentences that came through were fragmented, choppy, and sometimes scrambled.

He missed Mia so badly that it pained him to even think about her. He would imagine their times together, romantic walks in the Ozark hills and clear rushing streams of Arkansas. Despite their rare and fragmented communications, he knew that she was to give birth to their child next month, and it filled him with joy, despite the sadness of not being there with her. It gave him something to live for and a reason to do everything possible to get back home at the first opportunity. There had been talk of a rotation of pilots for months, but the intensity of the conflict meant that all B-21's would continue to be needed. The higher command wanted the aircraft to be on station near instantaneously and so they were against moving any of the aircraft back to the U.S.

Mark's hours were filled with moments of terror in his dreams and a growing guilt on his bombing runs. This was also mixed with an oddly comfortable and pleasant monotony, relaxing beneath the palm trees on the white sand beach near his officer quarters on Diego Garcia. Being a service member on an island fortress doesn't leave one with many options. All he could do was wait for his orders to change, and persistently work with the glitchy secure military e-mail system to try and communicate with his wife back home. The occasional success with the messages was enough to keep him strong mentally despite his growingly conflicted feelings about his mission. He was happy to find that Mia had moved in with her sister Ana and his brother-in-law Jacob. They were awesome people and he could only imagine the wonderful family times that they were experiencing together. Although he had no idea of when it would happen, he couldn't wait to join them and meet his first born child.

Chapter 20: The World Will Never Be the Same

In mid-March, a warmer day finally dawned with the promise of spring in the air, casting a warm and golden hue over Jacob and Ana's homestead. The gentle breeze was filled with the fresh scent of budding flowers and the lively chatter of songbirds that were just beginning to return from their winter sojourn. It was a day of renewal, a day when the world seemed to beckon them into its embrace.

It had been 3 weeks since they first heard of the conflict in India, but there had been very little internet connectivity since then, and Jacob believed that perhaps the frontlines had stabilized into a stalemate. Perhaps they would be spared from a nuclear apocalypse after all.

Jacob and Ana decided that it was time to allow their children to make their first foray of the year outside of the yard and barn areas. They would search for wild chives, fiddle heads (baby ferns), plantain greens, polk salad and perhaps a few early morel mushrooms. As they ventured into the forest, baskets in hand, the children skipped along the winding trails. Their laughter echoed through the trees, a joyful symphony that resonated with the spirit of the season. The younger ones eagerly hunted for spring mushrooms, while the older children gathered wild onions and greens for a salad, guided by the wisdom of their parents.

Ana's eyes sparkled with mirth as she watched their playful antics. She reveled in the simple pleasures of the day, the warmth of the sun on her skin, the earthy aroma of the woods, and the love and laughter of her family. *These moments, she thought, are the treasures that sustain us and make us push through the hard times.*

Jacob, ever the patient teacher, knelt down beside his youngest children. The twins, demonstrating how to identify edible mushrooms from their poisonous counterparts. He spoke in a gentle tone, instilling in them the knowledge passed down through generations. "Nature provides for us," he whispered to the children, "but we must learn to listen and to give thanks. Our labors to take care of God's creation are our way of giving thanks and this kind of work is our sacrifice. A sacrifice is a way of giving back to God."

The forest itself seemed to welcome their presence, its ancient trees swaying in silent approval. Shafts of sunlight pierced through the dense canopy, creating magical shifting patterns on the forest floor. Birds flitted through the branches, their songs weaving a tapestry of sound that echoed in harmony with the family's happiness.

Conversation flowed freely as they gathered their bounty. The children shared their dreams and aspirations, their innocent voices filled with hope for a future yet to unfold. Jacob junior was 11 now, and was talking of how he wanted to build a log cabin in the hidden valley below, and how Tommy, his new brother, would build another next to his own. Emma, at 8 years old, was going to teach herself to be a doctor, and invent new medicines for the animals and the people on the homestead. Jacob and Ana, who rarely had a break from homestead chores, listened and encouraged their children, their hearts swelling with pride for the resilient spirits they were nurturing.

Even Mia, who had been sad for months and desperately missed her husband, seemed more cheerful and even hopeful on this day. She was big and round from her pregnancy and she daydreamed about a time in the future when her own child would play with his cousins in the meadows and the forests of the homestead.

Lunch was a simple yet delicious affair, a salad crafted from the forest's offerings, as well as some deliciously salty deer jerky. They sat together on a patch of soft grass, savoring the flavors of the wild while basking in the love and camaraderie that enveloped them. The day felt like a reprieve from the harsh realities of the outside world, a moment suspended in time when nothing else mattered.

As the sun began its descent, casting a warm orange glow over the horizon, the family returned home, baskets brimming with their forest treasures, greens, a handful of mushrooms, a large deer antler "shed." The children's laughter and the echoes of their shared foray lingered in the pleasantly warm air, a testament to the enduring bonds of family and the unmatched beauty of nature.

Yet, as they sat together on their porch that evening, watching the stars twinkle to life in the darkening sky, a heaviness settled over Jacob. He knew that the world beyond their sanctuary was a dark storm, as if an evil akin to the mythical Mordor was growing by the minute, and he could sense that the tranquility of this day was a fragile respite from the tempest that continued to rage in the hearts of the rulers of nations.

Chapter 21: A Night Like no Other

A few weeks prior, Mia's husband, Major Mark Rinehart was having another nightmare. It was the same recurring dream in which he was frantically taking cover in the bombed out ruins of an Indian city, running from building to building, as tracers lit up the sky and missiles streaked through the night. Then he caught the glimpse of a cruise missile soaring above, and a bright flash in the distance, following by a blinding light and an overwhelming since of dread and imminent death. He jerked himself awake, and sat straight up, sweating even more profusely than the other nights. He immediately left his small quarters, descended the stairs to the ground level and walked the sandy path to the dark, moonlit beach. A navy shore patrol officer stopped him halfway. "Sailor where are you going?," demanded the officer. It was 2 A.M., local time, and no one was happy to be awake. There may have been a brutal war raging across the wide sea channel, but the servicemembers on Diego Garcia were downright indignant if you interrupted their sleep, their entertainment, or their meals.

"Settle down, sailor, I'm Major Rinehart, Air Force, I fly the B-21's." That shut the young sailor up immediately. No one messed with the pilots, they had a god-like status on the island. "Oh, I'm sorry sir," he gasped, saluting. Mark saluted back, and turned, walking away. Despite his troubled thoughts, he could not help but chuckle to himself as he walked away.

Here I am in boxer shorts, and the guy is saluting me like I'm General Colin Powell. This is unreal, sometimes I just love the Air Force.

He felt better and it was almost enough to make him turn and go back to his quarters, but the warm tropical night air was pleasant on his skin, and he knew that the water would be perfect so he continued to the beach. The water proved to be warmer and even calmer and more pleasant than usual. The tranquility of the sea and his restlessness led him to swim out further than he had ever gone before away from the shore. He was an excellent swimmer and the threat of sharks seemed trivial considering what he had been through. Before long he found himself perhaps 300 yards or more from the sandy beach.

The islands that make up Diego Garcia form an atoll that is sort of oval-shaped, with the land forming a thin ring around the large shallow sandy lagoon in the middle of the atoll. This ring of land is over 30 miles from top to bottom and half as wide. It has only one entrance for ships on the northern end, and Jacob's base was towards the middle, on the western side of the ring.

Jacob was swimming out towards the middle of this lagoon, one of the most beautiful places on Earth. Had it not been used for the war, this atoll would have likely been loaded with tourists, but instead, it was nearly deserted except for base personnel. Staring up at the night sky, Mark allowed himself a moment to picture his wife's face, imagining how she would look at this point in her pregnancy, and wondering what name she would pick for their child. Just then, Jacob spotted a bright shooting star streaking in from the north, and then oddly another shooting star emerging from that one.

DIEGO GARCIA

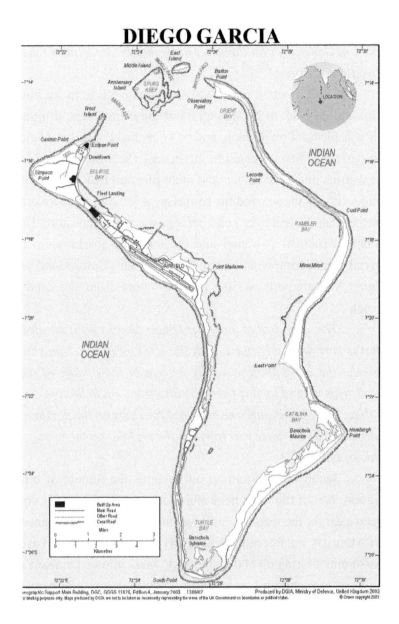

Map of Diego Garcia Atoll

With a sudden feeling of rising panic, he realized that to his dismay, it was not a shooting star at all, but instead, he now recognized it to be an advanced hypersonic cruise missile separating from its booster. From what he had been taught, these were used primarily by China and Russia, and were nuclear capable platforms. The streak was faster than almost any other missile that Mark had seen and in a matter of a few seconds, it descended almost like lightning from high in the sky down to Earth, directly towards the airfield, one half mile from his quarters and about almost one mile from his current location.

Mark was a helpless observer as he watched the impact in horror, but then suddenly remembering his training, decided to take a deep breath and submerge, in the case that it was an actual nuclear weapon. Once submerged, Mark forced himself to open his eyes under the salty water, using his arms to propel himself a few feet below the surface. Even beneath the surface, Mark could see and feel a deep impact and then the flash of a light so bright that it looked like the sun had descended from the sky directly on top of the military island. He could even feel the intense heat through the water and fought to propel himself deeper and hold his breath as long as possible. He tried to remain calm so as not to raise his heart rate and in this way, preserve the oxygen in his lungs.

Thinking quickly, Mark, still underwater, removed his boxer shorts, his only piece of clothing other than dog tags. He put the boxer shorts over his head, and emerged slightly from the hot surface water to gasp for another breath of air, feeling as if he was breathing air from the open door of a hot baking oven, and filling his lungs as full as possible before re-submerging. He had gone through plenty of survival training and was an expert swimmer, but had never even imagined a scenario like this. Going back beneath the water, Mark was processing the fact that a nuclear weapon had indeed just gone off, destroying the Air Base, his quarters, his plane, and all of his friends and squadron members. It was a gut-wrenching realization, but he knew that survival was his first priority. He had been carrying with him the sacred responsibility that he was going to be a father soon, and there was no higher calling for him at this moment than to get back home to his family. Mark emerged again, face covered, relieved to find that the brightness had largely passed, though the location of his base was still one brightly glowing mass, and the air around him, while still hot, was much cooler, than before.

He decided to submerge once more, just for good measure, managing to hold his breath for probably another 60 seconds.

Mark had been raised Catholic, but had not felt much of a spiritual connection since the time that he graduated from his Catholic High School, in Columbia, Missouri. But, in this moment, as he emerged the third time from the water and felt the slight bit of coolness from an odd, rushing breeze from the East, he could not help but to pause, his eyes still closed, and tears beginning to flow down his already wet cheeks, as he slowly recited a prayer that he had not heard or spoken, for years, "Glory be to the Father, and the Son, and the Holy Spirit, As it was in the beginning, is now, and ever shall be, world without end. Amen."

Marks face then shifted from one of humble supplication to a hard-jawed look of determination, as he said to himself, "Okay Marcus, let's do this," and the man, without looking back at the glowing scene of destruction behind him, turned east, and begin swimming to the opposite side of the atoll.

Chapter 22: Anguish and Joy on the Homestead

Back on the Homestead, the entire family was just returning to the house from one of their food gathering trips to the forest. The peace that they all experienced from their forest adventures had been revitalizing, but on this day, upon their return, the peace quickly gave way to shock and dismay as Jacob checked the internet, finding that it was functioning for the first time in weeks. The headlines screamed warnings to take cover, and the outside world they had known was unraveling before their eyes. A nuclear war, possibly limited, possibly not, had erupted, and the news was a chilling litany of destruction and despair.

In a stunning turn of events, it was India that was being blamed for igniting the powder keg, unleashing a tactical nuclear bomb upon the remote and strategic island of Diego Garcia. The reports from the region provided chilling specifics, painting a picture of escalating hostilities across multiple fronts. India found itself in the middle of the harrowing face-off, not only against its regional rivals China and Pakistan but also against the United States, who increasingly was being seen as doing the bidding of the CCP in China. The world was now a geopolitical minefield, poised on the brink of further catastrophe. Surprisingly, it initially seemed that only one tactical nuke had been launched and the other forces in the area had paused operations and not yet retaliated.

World leaders had not held back verbally, and their words reverberated in the global consciousness. The Prime

Minister of India, in a sternly delivered address, asserted, "We deny involvement in the bombing of Diego Garcia, but have defended our sovereignty and will not bow to foreign aggression. The world must recognize our right to exist and also protect our interests at any cost." His counterpart in Pakistan issued an equally resolute response, declaring, "Pakistan stands united against external interference. We will counter Indian aggression and then some, whatever the consequences." It seemed a cut and dry case, India had received the brunt of American attacks, and so they would be the most likely culprit to have hit back at the air base in Diego Garcia. Russia had been an ally of India in the conflict, but was not being named as a suspect. Jacob found it odd that no one was asking if perhaps India had been framed. After all, India also had the most to lose by striking U.S. Forces so aggressively.

Across the Pacific, President Robert Williams of the United States did not hesitate to place all of the blame on India, addressing the nation with conviction. "At this moment our thoughts and our prayers must be with the families of the service men and women that were stationed on the island of Diego Garcia. We will investigate the source of the tactical nuke, and our response will be swift and uncompromising. We are more resolved than ever to defend our allies and interests in the region," he declared. "We are prepared to use all means necessary to protect American lives and assets abroad and if it is found that India is the culprit, then our response will be overwhelming and merciless." His words echoed the rising anger of a nation that had until recently been on the verge of collapse. It was the first hint of unity that Americans had felt in over a decade.

The government censored media was also obscuring the fact that over 10 million Americans had died from starvation or exposure over the brutal winter. Despite their suffering, Americans were now willing to give up their freedom indefinitely to guarantee their security. Emergencies are good tools for making people give up their rights willingly.

The president continued, "Today I announce the extension of martial law into the indefinite future. I have ordered my cabinet secretaries to partner with our generals at the pentagon to nationalize all remaining military-supporting infrastructure to include petroleum production, defense-related manufacturing, and production of food and staples. I am also permanently nationalizing our national guard forces and state law enforcement agencies, who will seamlessly be integrated into our military command structure. FOR THE GREATER GOOD, this integrated command structure will bring about an orderly transition from the chaos of the past to the efficiency and prosperity that we all need right now. At the same time, any nuclear action by a foreign enemy will be answered by retaliation in kind. Thanks to all loyal Americans for their continued support of THE GREATER GOOD. This terrible deed will not go unpunished!"

There was even a staged crowd listening to the president's address, chanting and echoing him every time he said "For the Greater Good!" Jacob even noticed a strange banner with a sort of modified American flag, right up next to the president. It had the stars in the middle and stripes in a hexagon around the outsides.

Jacob was incredulous. The president is using even the outbreak of nuclear war as an excuse to grab more power. Everything is an excuse to grab power.

———————

Mia had retreated into the barn and asked to have some time alone. Jacob and Ana had learned to respect her boundaries while they all lived in such close quarters. At the same time, they knew that it was critical to stay informed and so they continued to follow newscasts intently from the safety of their underground home.

On the global stage, world leaders grappled with the rapidly escalating crisis. UN Secretary-General Maria Lopez implored, "The world stands at the precipice of an unimaginable catastrophe. I call upon all parties to exercise restraint and seek a peaceful resolution before it is too late." Her pleas were echoed by leaders from nations near and far, but the tensions and assumed retaliation seemed unstoppable.

Before, they could even finish watching the interview of the U.N. Secretary General, headlines began popping up that the U.S. had already launched retaliatory strikes likely from submarines, due to the fact that the air base and all air assets and personnel on Diego Garcia had been destroyed. Jacob and Ana could only watch in disbelief, a nuclear war in their lifetimes. How many people had said this would never happen again? Now that it had started, how far would it go? Would it remain on the other side of the world?

Ana went to comfort Mia and bring her back to the warmth of the home. Mia's pregnancy was now full term and Ana was worried that the baby could come at any moment. More than anything, she wanted to keep an eye on her sister, and keep her safe, especially if she suddenly went into labor. Ana comforted her by telling her, "Mia do you remember the old man in our village, named Damjan in our village?" Mia nodded and Ana continued, "Damjan was 16 years old when the Nazis came through and conscripted him and the other men in our village to fight on the side of the axis in WWII. They took them all to fight in Stalingrad in the winter of 1942 and 43. Damjan and all the others were given up as lost and believed dead. Three years later, he came walking back into the village on his own two feet, even though he was missing a few toes to frost bite."

"But the other men died, what are the odds of survival?," protested Mia, becoming more upset.

"SHHH!!," Ana, warned her, assertively, grasping her sister by the shoulders and looking into her eyes, "Listen to me, what if you die because you can't get it together mentally? And then, Mark comes walking up our driveway in a few months. He is probably out there fighting to get home right now, and his only hope is that you are here waiting for him. Now, be strong! Damjan survived Stalingrad, our father survived the massacre at Vukovar. You found a good man in Mark and he is coming home, so you get strong right now!"

Mia nodded at her sister, still fighting back tears, wiping her nose. "You're right, you're right!," responded Mia. "I am going to see him again, and I want him to see his child." The two sisters embraced and started to relax. Soon they were chatting about baby names, a welcome respite from all the worrying that they had done in these days. It was a comfortable Mid-April night, and there was no gunfire, no strange lights in the sky, and no sign of the chaos that was taking place on the other side of the world. They smiled and laughed as they walked back down to the house. Ana and Jacob agreed to monitor reports throughout the night, in case they needed to take cover from a potential nuclear counterattack. It was a sleepless night but the adults tried to get some rest, in order to be ready for difficult days ahead.

———————

In the morning, Mia was visibly sick, pale, and unable to eat or hold down food. She lay in bed in a separate room while Ana and Jacob made cold breakfast cereal with goat milk for the children. After breakfast, Jacob took Ana up to the cupola to tell her what he had gathered from the initial reports. He told her that the epicenter of the retaliatory devastation lay in the populous cities of southern India. The initial estimates of civilian casualties were staggering, with figures soaring into the tens of millions. News reports painted a haunting picture of entire cities reduced to rubble, with survivors left to grapple with unspeakable loss and suffering. There was also a realization that in most areas, there would be no rescue due to a lack of remaining infrastructure. It was possible that this conflict may see a billion people wiped off the face of the planet in very short order. The only glimmer of hope was that the nuclear conflict might stay limited, and perhaps there would be no nuclear winter or no direct conflict in the continental United States.

Jacob also informed Ana that the news reports mentioned that the U.S. had launched what they were calling a limited nuclear strike from submarines, and it was implied that the American aircraft and air force squadrons on Diego Garcia had been wiped out. They would shield the news from Mia for the time being. It was important for her not to lose hope, especially now that her baby might arrive any day now.

They had made preparations for the worst but chores still had to be done. Life would go on in their corner of the world, and they would constantly pray that the nuclear conflict would not spread further. After checking on and feeding the goats and chickens, as well as the dog Max, Ana and Jacob returned to the house. They could see that the children had been whispering and were worried about their aunt Mia. Ana, ever resilient and resourceful, took charge of the younger children. She gathered them close, shielding them from the grim reality that had suddenly shattered their world. With whispered words of comfort and a loving embrace, she did her best to maintain a sense of normalcy amid the chaos. She took them into the kitchen and helped them get a board game started to take their minds off the situation. Mental preparedness was at least as important as everything else in times like these.

The evening deepened into a darkness that seemed to mirror the uncertainty that had now shrouded their future. The internet and all communications were out now. They didn't even have Bill to communicate with anymore on the GMRS radio. It was as if 200 years of technology had been swept away and they were no longer part of modern society. Instead, they were left with nothing between them and nature, themselves, and God's creation. As if there was no outside world, no terrible war beyond the horizon, no martial law and no draconian state taking hold in their country. It was a warm night so they huddled together, seeking solace in each other's presence. The stars were brighter than ever, as power outages in the surrounding area were nearly constant. The world had irrevocably changed, and the question on their minds was if they had actually done enough to prepare. It was them vs. fate, and the laws of nature as well as the laws of war, that would determine their future. They slept well that night, even Mia, with no news from the outside world. Even the dog Max had nothing to bark at on that quiet, cloudless, unusually warm April night.

———————

The next morning, Mia's distress was almost unbearable, and it was clearly visible to the others. But today, she no longer looked pale. Instead, her face was slightly swollen and her pupils seemed large, she almost looked ready to do battle. Ana and Jacob had not had time to make breakfast or begin chores, when they noticed that Mia might need some assistance. Mia moved out of her bed in the saferoom, holding young Emma's hand and carrying her large pregnant belly over to the kitchen table when a wave of pain shot through her. She gasped, her grip on Emma tightening involuntarily. "Ouch, Aunt Mia!" squeaked Emma, surprised. "Sorry sweety," answered Mia, now taking a seat. Jacob, ever watchful, noticed her distress immediately.

"Mia!" he exclaimed, concern etched across his face as he rushed to her side. "Ana, it's happening. We need to help her."

Ana, always composed in the face of adversity, nodded in understanding. She quickly ushered the younger children into the safe room, where the muted glow of an old DVD playing on the laptop kept them busy while the adults dealt with more urgent matters. With instructions for the older children to stay calm and take care of their little siblings, she closed but didn't lock the reinforced door behind her, keeping them in the safe room.

Meanwhile, Mia's contractions were intensifying, each one more excruciating than the last. She clenched her jaw, tears streaming down her face, as she struggled to maintain her composure. Jacob, ever the pillar of strength, helped her to a makeshift birthing area that they had prepared in the adjacent bedroom.

"Deep breaths, Mia," Ana urged, her voice unwavering. "We're here for you. You can do this. You are going to meet your little one soon."

Ana, having delivered her own children, was ready and eager to assist. She provided comfort, guidance, and medical supplies that they had stored for such emergencies. The hours that followed were a whirlwind of pain, determination, and love. Mia's strength shone through as she brought a new life into the world, with Jacob and Ana's unwavering support.

Inside the safe room, the children huddled together, their eyes glued to their movie, a rare treat, and they barely noticed that their aunt was in labor. During a pause between contractions, Ana assured the children that their aunt would be okay, and they barely looked up. "Let us know when we can play with our new cousin," said Emma, matter-of-factly.

As Mia labored, her strength waned and her breaths grew labored. But with every contraction, her determination to bring her child safely into the world burned brighter. Jacob and Ana provided unwavering support, their hands steady, their voices soothing. It was a testament to the strength of their family and a reminder that even in the darkest of times, life found a way to persist.

Outside the safety of their homestead, the world continued to unravel. In the days prior, they had seen images of devastation and suffering, each scene a stark reminder of the fragility of human existence. But within their small, resilient world that they had built over the years, a new life was entering the world, a symbol of hope in a time of despair.

And as the cries of the newborn baby filled the air, a profound sense of wonder and gratitude washed over them all. It was a fragile moment of beauty amidst the chaos, a reminder that life, in all its complexity, was worth protecting and cherishing, no matter the circumstances.

Chapter 23: New Life on the Homestead

Mia's new baby boy, Damjan Rinehart, was just over 8 lbs., a large feat for a first time mother, but the natural home birth had gone as well as could be hoped for, and Mia was walking on her own within an hour of giving birth. Life on the homestead continued despite the looming specter of the nuclear conflict that raged outside their secluded haven. Mia, her newborn baby in her arms, felt an unexpected and unjustified sense of confidence that she would see her husband again, and that Mark would see his baby boy someday. Her heart ached for her husband, but she felt that a piece of him was with her already as she held baby Damjan in her arms. The new life was the embodiment of the love between the couple, and she would wait for her man for as long as it took for him to come back to her from the far side of the world.

Jacob, Ana, and the rest of the family carried on with their daily chores and preparations. Spring had finally arrived, and they couldn't afford to falter in their self-sufficiency. The cattle, goats, and chickens still required attention, and their garden had been started and so was in need of water, weeding, and fertilizing. All of the blood from the recently butchered animals as well as crushed bones and feathers, had been kept to be applied as a fertilizer to the garden, and it was already starting to show promise. Jacob, years ago, had built several raised beds that were 32 inches high, and this comfortable height made the chore of gardening feel like a fun hobby.

Ana also was managing homeschooling the children, maintaining a sense of normalcy amidst the chaos beyond their homestead. Twins, Sarah and Michael, were now five and beginning to read their first books. Books of all kinds were one of the items that the couple had stockpiled over the years. Jacob, 11 years old, loved history, and he would read one history book after the next; very thirsty for knowledge. Emma, now 9 was most fond of reading about living things, and she liked to study not only their livestock, but all of the living and growing things on their farm. She was already picking up on the ways that one organism depended on another. She had been fascinated at how the blood, bones, and feathers from the butchered animals were now essential for the growth of the plants in their garden. She wanted to learn about all of the micronutrients and microorganisms that were involved in the process. Jacob and Ana knew that their children had a natural curiosity about the world, and rather than try to give them curiosity, they just had to make sure that they as parents didn't crush it.

The family worked tirelessly to ensure that their provisions would last, rationing their supplies and stretching their resources. Ana and Jacob meticulously tended to their food stores, making every can of preserved vegetables, every bag of rice, and every jar of pickles count. In the evenings, they had reorganized the supplies, putting things in order of expiration date, checking for air-tight seals, and identifying anything that was spoiled to be given to the chickens or the dog. The goats were very sensitive to anything moldy and so they were only given fresh hay in the winter. Now that it was spring, they could finally forage again. Ana and Jacob knew they couldn't rely on the outside world for sustenance any longer, perhaps never again.

Their root cellar, once filled with the bounty of last year's harvest, had all winter been a treasure trove of preserved vegetables, potatoes, and fruits. It was a testament to their foresight and hard work. The children often accompanied their parents on trips to the cellar, marveling at the shelves lined with jars and containers. They explained to the children that because it was now springtime, they would be working hard for the next several months to fill their cellar, their treasure room, with the crops of this new year!

Each family member had their role to play. The children, now more than ever, needed to be self-reliant. They learned the art of planting seeds, tending to young plants, and the importance of crop rotation throughout the raised beds. Every day, they ventured into the garden, gaining valuable skills that might one day be essential for their survival. It was their playground.

Their livestock, too, required the care of the entire family. Feeding the animals, cleaning their pens, and milking the goats had become a daily routine. The goats provided both milk and meat, a renewable resource that the family couldn't afford to squander. Ana took pride in her ability to manage the animals, her hands skilled from years of practice. Now that the pastures were beginning to grow, the older boys, Jake and his adopted brother Tommy would take the goats for most of the day down the hill, across the creek, and away from the county road in order to get them fresh green forage, which the goats needed to replenish their bodies' stores of vitamins and nutrients, after eating hay all winter. The boys loved their days serving as shepherds. They would play as hunters and soldiers, sneaking up on each other and practicing the art of camouflage and stealth. Occasional Emma, now 9 years old would go with them, but they often played rougher than she liked. She enjoyed picking wildflowers and feeding them to the goats, taking notes about which plants the goats preferred.

Despite the uncertainty and anxiety that plagued the world around them, the family found solace in their unity and self-sufficiency. The homestead was their sanctuary, a place where they could shelter from the storms of the outside world. Each day brought new challenges, but they faced them together, relying on their family bonds and resourcefulness to thrive in an ever-changing landscape.

Mia spent much of her time lost in the new love that she had found with her new baby boy, Damjan, who was strong and healthy from the beginning. He was an amazing blessing and Mia found it miraculous to already see her husband's loving brown eyes and kind expressions in the baby's face. Still, despite her determination to hold out hope and believe that her husband would return, serious doubts had begun to creep into her mind. It had been weeks now since the destruction of the base on Diego Garcia and there had not been any internet nor cellular service. There was no information available at all, and she tried to put it out of her mind.

The entire family felt the uncertainty about the outside world but felt blessed every single day by the coming of a beautiful spring and the nature that was all around them at the homestead. They held onto the hope that their watchful eyes and unwavering determination would see them through the darkest of times.

Chapter 24: Turtle Cove

Jacob faced a three mile swim to get across the lagoon in the middle of the night, from the airfield side to the uninhabited eastern part of the atoll. There was a bright unknown star in the clear eastern sky, opposite the air base, and Mark would glance up occasionally to make sure he was heading in the direction of that star. The ring shaped island's central lagoon area was tranquil water, and Mark had been on the swim team at his high school, so it was a fairly easy feat. He did not stop to give himself time to grieve, but instead, was determined to survive, conjuring up images in his mind from the story of Beowulf, the great swimmer, who would wrestle sea monsters and live to tell the tale. After about an hour and a half of steady swimming and a huge effort, Mark arrived at a place called East Point, wearily dragging himself up onto the beach in the darkness, muscles throbbing but feeling strong, nonetheless. The air was pleasant and felt warm like a blanket compared to the water of the lagoon, and he laid flat on his back on the hard wet sand, catching his breath. After less than a minute, Mark noticed something bad, it was very bad. There was an almost transparent, light ashy substance falling from the sky, in small, barely visible particles that could be seen just barely catching the ambient light, and almost unnoticeable on his bare skin.

No, no, no, it's nuclear fallout! This is the worst case scenario; I am downwind from nuclear fallout.

Mark rushed back into the ocean, dunking himself under the water in an attempt to wash off any unseen particles. Only then did he finally take a moment to look at the blaze in the distance that was once a military base and airfield. It was glowing hot in the sky, and secondary explosions had finally died down. Other than the fire, it was eerily quiet. The magnitude of the blast meant that no rescue crew, no fire department, and no emergency team would be left on the island to attempt to rescue survivors, and survivors were unlikely in any case. Mark had barely been able to raise his head above the water to breathe after the blast due to the extreme heat. Looking at the eastern shore where he had just arrived, he noticed that all of the palm trees and other vegetation had not burned, but they were uprooted and flattened straight down to the ground, tops facing away from the blast.

It was only then that Mark fully realized how lucky or perhaps how blessed he had truly been. Now wading neck-deep in the water, he surmised that he was likely the only survivor on almost the entire atoll, unless someone else had been swimming underwater, or staying on the southernmost, uninhabited part of the island, or maybe in a bunker. But there was no warning and no air raid siren. No type of missile had successfully struck the base in the past so no one expected anything like this ever to happen. The base felt like an unreachable fortress in the middle of the sea.

Judging from the flattened but not incinerated trees where he was, three miles from the detonation, Mark estimated that they had been hit by a tactical nuke of about 50 kilotons. This was about the maximum payload for a hypersonic weapon such as a Russian Kinzhal missile, with which Mark was familiar with because of his advanced military education, including his years at the Air Force Academy. There many naval vessels nearby but it was unlikely that naval commanders would approach near to the island for fear of exposing their sailors to radiation in an area where survivors were highly unlikely. Mark felt no anger at whomever was responsible. Their mission had become so murky, with so many sinister foreign forces involved, that he had no idea who was to blame, nor did he care.

Instead, Major Rinehart was determined to survive and to see his beloved Mia and his child whom he had never met, and so he resolved to start swimming south, still inside the ring-shaped island, inside the lagoon. Walking would have been easier, even without shoes, but he knew that it was much safer to avoid the radioactive fallout debris by swimming in the ocean instead of going by land. Constantly rinsing himself with seawater while swimming might be a way to completely avoid radiation sickness. He knew that the atoll and thus the lagoon was over 30 miles from north to south, and he estimated that he was still 10 miles from the southern point of the lagoon. At the southern point was a beautiful place called "Turtle Cove." Swimming three miles had been difficult, and swimming another ten miles seemed a truly inhuman feat, at least for him. It would take at least 6 hours, which by his estimates would get him there by almost noon the following day. If he could make it to Turtle Cove, then the effects of the radiation and radioactive fallout would likely be minimal. It was his best hope and he had to try. To make it easier, he planned to follow the coastline and occasionally swim to the shallow areas to take a rest.

Hours later, the tropical sun began to climb high into the cloudless sky above the Diego Garcia atoll. White sand beaches ringed the blue lagoon, but the seagulls, fish, and other signs of life were nowhere to be found. There was only one man, naked, swimming south along the edge of the white beach, skin beginning to burn in the rising sun. Major Rinehart was reaching the limits of what his body could do, having no food or water in more than 15 hours and having swam nearly 13 miles straight with few breaks. He had been a competitive swimmer in high school, years earlier, but this was over five times the distance that had to be swum in an ironman competition.

By the time Mark's fingers finally touched the white sand from the beach at turtle cove, the southern tip of the atoll, he was dizzy, beginning to experience heat exhaustion and tunnel vision, and the light of the day seemed to pulse in his vision as he struggled to get up on to his knees, and then to an upright stance at the edge of the beach.

C'mon Marcus, you have made it, this is no time to collapse, just a little further. This is what you were made for, you were made for struggle, for challenge, this is your sacrifice, your time to show fortitude.

He looked around trying to orient himself, relieved to finally see an area where most of the trees were upright, instead of being blown over by the blast. He found some shade at the interior edge of the beach, finally able to get out of the sun for the first time that day. Luckily the blast of wind from the nuclear explosion had not reached this far south, meaning that his assumption that it had been a tactical nuclear explosion, was correct. He also did not see any visible nuclear fallout debris, another Godsend. There was, however, a large amount of random debris in the lagoon, most likely from a combination of the initial nuclear blast, and the strong winds generated by the explosion. Mark decided to kneel but on one knee, for fear that if he sat, or got comfortable, then he might drift off and sleep. He knew that what he really needed was fresh water.

After a quick rest, Mark was back on his feet in less than a minute, his head beginning to throb with dehydration, the daylight flickering as it filtered through the tree branches above his head. He knew that he needed water, and he needed it soon if he wanted to avoid passing out. Luckily, he had visited this area of the beach with some of the other pilots from his squadron, on one of their morning runs. He normally didn't like to run even half this far, but when they were all new to the base and the island, they had been eager to explore the area. On their adventure, they had been to this very spot, and Mark remembered noticing a small pond or miniature lagoon, only 100 meter across, that he believed contained fresh water.

Scanning the coastline, he spotted an area up ahead, outside of the lagoon and closer to the southern side, nearer to the ocean. The area was distinct in that there was a break in the trees and an apparent low spot in the land. Mark set off in that direction with high hopes. He had forgotten about being completely naked as he had even lost his boxer shorts at this point. The small shrubs scratched his calves and ankles but he failed to notice because of his dehydration-induced tunnel vision and his need to focus on navigating to the low point in the terrain, just 150 yards away.

Finally, the mini lagoon came into focus. He stumbled up to the edge, which like most of the island, was another sandy beach. Mark knew that there could be dangerous pathogens in the water so he quickly and instinctively dug a hole in the sand, roughly three feet from the water. It was clean sand, and not a perfect solution, but the water that drained from the lagoon into the hole would at least have a chance to be sand filtered at least from larger sized pathogens. After the hole was dug, water actually began seeping in, very slowly, but steadily, it had worked! It was a long five minute wait for the water to fill up the hole with perhaps 1 gallon of water, and then Mark laid flat on his belly, slurping up the water like a cow, with his head as far into the hole as he could reach. It was fresh and the best water that he had ever tasted in his life!

After drinking his fill, Mark could finally start to more clearly survey the strip of land, which appeared to be between a quarter and a half mile across from the central saltwater lagoon on the inside, to the Indian Ocean on the outside. Mark walked the remaining distance to the Indian ocean side, about 800 feet further south past the freshwater lagoon to survey the vast expanse of the Indian Ocean, and the beautiful white sand beach that stretched in an arc around the outside of the atoll. Straining his eyes to look far to the north, he spotted a small dark unknown object on the beach at the edge of the ocean water. It almost looked like a raft, parked near a grove of coconut trees. He estimated the possible raft to be only 600 yards away, and he knew that about 3 miles past that location, further north there was a munitions storage facility. If there were survivors, perhaps they would be at the munitions storage area.

Major Rinehart began walking north along the beach at a brisk pace, with hopes for a quick rescue from his predicament. His sunburn was probably getting serious by now, walking barefoot and naked along the beach, but it was the least of his worries. As he approached within about 100 yards, he could now clearly make out a large black raft, resembling a military Zodiac boat with a large engine on the back, it was clear that the boat was intentionally moored and he was almost sure to be rescued. As he continued to approach, he could now spot one individual nearby, who oddly appeared to have olive drab pants, and a blue shirt, and maybe a blue hat or a beret on his head?

Strange, no one wears berets on tactical missions; who wears blue hats, he thought to himself. Jeez who cares Marcus, do you want to be rescued or not? Let's make some new friends and get the hell out of here on that boat.

Just as Mark was about to start waving his arms and yelling towards his potential rescuer, he began to hear gunfire a few miles to the north, probably in the vicinity of the large munitions depot, where both the Air Force and the Navy had stockpiled all sorts of munitions, possibly even nuclear warheads mounted to cruise missiles. Mark quickly ducked into the thicket at the inner edge of the beach, still undetected by the man with the blue hat. He then approached stealthily closer to the man, soon 50 yards away then 25. The gunfire started, stopped, and picked up again far in the distance. Now, Mark could hear the man singing through the trees, but not in English.

Mark had studied Russian at the Air Force academy, and he immediately recognized the song was in Russian, and the man sounded a little drunk. Mark peaked around the tree to glance at the man closer, now making out a thin soldier with sunburnt skin and light hair, wearing camouflage pants, a baby blue striped t-shirt and a blue beret that clearly identified him as being part of the Russian Special Forces or Spetsnaz. He had his AK-47 leaned up against the tree behind him and he was nursing a flask of alcohol, probably vodka, as he sang and gestured at the sky. His right hand was holding the flask and he had a cigarette in his left, leaning back, using the palm tree as his lounge chair. Mark ducked behind the tree again. He had to think this through, it was a hugely surprising turn of events.

Holy crap, thought Mark, of course the Russians would send an actual Spetsnaz patrol to do a damage assessment after a tactical nuclear strike. Or maybe there was something in the munitions area that the Russians wanted, more nukes? American-made nukes? Of course. And only a Russian would take the opportunity to get drunk while guarding the boat for his comrades. Well Marcus, you need that boat, and it looks like Vladimir's drunken holiday is about to come to an end.

Mark's senses were heightened as he crept up through the dense stand of trees, silently approaching the man from his blind spot to the rear, inch by inch. It was too easy and suddenly Mark was at the man's tree! He grabbed the AK that was leaned up the tree, and raised it up over his shoulder to prepare a powerful blow from the butt of the rifle, "Kak Dela Comrade (What's Up)?," said the man in Russian, sensing his presence. But it was too late, Mark powerfully slammed the butt of the rifle into the man's temple, knocking him to the ground, unconscious. Major Rinehart was a pilot, but he had trained for combat for many years, and showed no mercy. He slammed the back end of that rifle against the man's head repeatedly, until blood began to ooze from the Russian's nostrils and the man's skull began to take on an increasingly flattened shape.

Enough Marcus, you have killed once again. This isn't the same as killing from 30,000 feet. It feels more like a deer hunt or a boxing match, yeah, this man had it coming. I've killed hundreds maybe thousands with my bombs, and this is the first justified kill of my life, Lord forgive me, I am the worst kind of murderer. Oh God, please with thy loving kindness blot out my transgressions and deliver me from this evil.

Mark was frozen in the moment, but quickly shook his head, snapping out of the emotion, "Let's get serious, this is my one chance!," he said to himself out loud. It was a risk but Mark noticed that the man was almost exactly his size, so he took the time to drag him into the boat, which was only 20 feet away. It was the quickest way to hide the body from the rest of the man's comrades and also take his clothes for his own use, as protection from the scorching tropical sun. He also put the rifle in the boat.

Within 5 minutes, Mark had dispatched the Russian soldier, thrown him in the rubber boat, pushed off from the shore and started the diesel engine. No one had discovered his presence, so he was free to take his time quickly getting familiar with how to maneuver the rubber boat, steering it by grabbing onto the tiller handle attached to the engine, that also served as a throttle. It was easy to figure out and in no time, Mark had the boat turned towards the open ocean and was quickly putting distance between himself and the shore. Within less than 10 minutes, the shore was no longer visible, and Mark heard a large explosion, looking back over his shoulder just in time to see what appeared to be rockets or other munitions cooking off and streaking into the sky from what he had estimated to be the location of the large American ammunition storage area. Jacob throttled down to a stop, keeping the engine idling, the shore no longer visible and the waves beginning to toss him a bit from side to side in the boat. He quickly removed the dead man's clothes and put them on his own sore, sunburnt body. The boots were just a bit large but better than nothing. He also noticed a phrase in Russian on a pendant with the man's dog tags. It read, "Tem Bol'Sheye Blago," meaning "for the greater good." He then easily shoved the young Russian's skinny body over the side of the raft muttering the phrase, "Requiesce in Pace."

Looking around him, Major Mark Rinehart felt truly small. He was a tiny speck in an immense, rough, and merciless ocean. He could count on no help from others. To his rear, towards the East, was his former Air Base, destroyed by a tactical nuke. Somewhere there were ships from the U.S. Navy but they had surely moved locations after the nuke had detonated. In addition, there were apparently Russian forces in the area, perhaps Indian forces, and maybe even the Chinese. He noticed that there were rubberized containers in the boat potentially filled with food and water, and was happy to find 5 full fuel cans as well, perhaps 30 gallons. There was no time to inspect further, he grasped the tiller of the boat's engine once again, throttling up aggressively and he began navigating based on the arc of the sun. He steered the boat directly west and towards the uncertain prospect of the continent of Africa. It would be a long journey, but Mark was determined to reach his home, the love of his life, Mia, and their newborn child.

To Be Continued

Buy My Non-Fiction book and be prepared for anything, just like Jacob and Ana! This book gives more background on the actual real-life scenarios that everyone should strive to be prepared for. It also gives detailed instructions on how to be more self-sufficient and prepare every aspect of your homestead for any catastrophe, including security, energy, water, food, shelter, and much more.

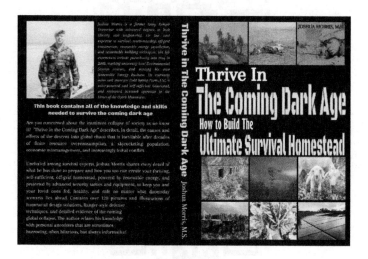

SCAN HERE!

SCAN HERE!
For My Youtube Channel

SCAN HERE!
For My Preparedness
and Homesteading
Facebook Group

Printed in Great Britain
by Amazon

44385011R00128